The River Capture

D0111471

'Costello plays with the borders of psychological realism in this ruminative, dream-like novel, which sweeps up ideas about animal rights, the legacy of trauma, the fluidity of sexual experience and the purpose of art itself within the fragmenting, restlessly questioning perceptions of one man's gradual breakdown'
Metro

'Mary Costello, with the sharp spade of *The River Capture*, made Joyce turn in his grave in Zurich, in a good way'
Sebastian Barry, *Irish Independent*

'One of the most intriguing works by an Irish writer since Mike McCormack's *Solar Bones* . . . Full of tenderness, beauty and some deeply affecting human introspection'
Sunday Independent

'Deft and elegant, earthy and immersing, *The River Capture* is a searingly close portrait of a protagonist unravelling. The legacy of Joyce, family secrets, duty and desire, hope and loneliness are the strands that wind through Luke's story. The result is utterly compelling'
Jess Kidd

Also by Mary Costello

Academy Street
The China Factory

The
River
Capture

Mary Costello

CANONGATE

This paperback published in 2020 by Canongate Books

First published in Great Britain in 2019 by Canongate Books Ltd,
14 High Street, Edinburgh EH1 1TE

canongate.co.uk

I

This is a work of fiction. It is not based on real events, people or places. Any resemblance
to actual persons or events is entirely coincidental.

The River Capture received financial assistance from the Arts Council of Ireland

British Library Cataloguing-in-Publication Data
A catalogue record for this book is available on
request from the British Library

ISBN 978 1 78689 804 3

Typeset in Centaur MT by Palimpsest Book Production Ltd, Falkirk, Stirlingshire

Printed and bound in Great Britain by Clays Ltd, Elcograf S.p.A.

For
Martin

'In theory, there is a gravitational attraction between every drop of sea water and even the outermost star of the universe.'

Rachel Carson

BAREFOOT, LUKE O'BRIEN descends the stairs of Ardboe House and stands at the window on the return landing. All Waterford around him: fertile fields, ancient oak forests, a great river plain, a castle three miles away with other ancestral houses spread out like satellites around it, and, less than a quarter of a mile away as the crow flies, the bend in the Sullane river and on its far bank the town of Clonduff.

A fine morning. Lynch's cattle are spread out in Luke's fields, calm after last night's racket. A single cloud approaches the sun. At intervals between the oak and beech trees on the riverbank, water birds skim the surface and the river glints in the sunlight. Before descending the remaining stairs Luke inhales the cool air of the house and waits for the cloud to pass.

He crosses the hall, deep red carpet underfoot, and opens the front door. The cat darts past and runs ahead of him, tail in the air, down the back hall into the kitchen. Kitten belly on her again, he thinks. You old slut, Lily. He rubs her ears. She meows loudly, snaking between his legs as he opens a tin of cat food. Need to get you spayed, missy, he says.

In the downstairs bathroom he empties his bladder. *Mingo*. He wishes he had learned Latin. He'd like to be able to conjugate verbs, recognise instantly the Latin root of a word. He stands before the mirror. Something like the rumble of thunder woke him at 2 a.m. When he looked out, Lynch's cattle were mounting each other under the full moon. Uncastrated bulls, weighing nearly a ton each, Lynch's latest enterprise. They thrive far better, he told Luke, and have a higher kill-out percentage at the factory. Last night they were demented. One by one they pawed the ground, lowered their heads and thundered down towards the river.

He examines his teeth, checks his crown. He'll be bald before he's forty, like Dadda. Nothing between me and Heaven, Dadda used to say. Hirsute arms and legs, a bit of grey in his temples. He lathers on shaving foam and begins to shave. The short strokes of the Bic razor rasp against his skin. He once slept with a girl from Rathgar who had white pubic hair, and she only twenty-five. *Fernfoils of maidenhair*. Was that Stephen or Bloom? More like Bloom, he thinks. Josie went bald down there, but he thinks that was from the chemo. In her final months he used to take her to the toilet, bathe her. His strange, simple-minded aunt. She had more baths and showers in the last six months of her life than she had in the sixty-six years that went before.

The kitchen sink is piled with dirty dishes, pots and

pans, cutlery. He begins to sort them, scraping grease and mould from the saucepans into the bin. Then, frustrated, he gives up. He takes the tea towel from the little rubber suction hook, sniffs it, then tosses it away. He read somewhere that dishcloths are two hundred thousand times dirtier than toilet seats. That couldn't be right, could it? His eyes are drawn to spots of mould on the grout between the tiles where the tea towel hung. Microbes, colonies of bacteria dividing and multiplying there in the dark under his nose for years. Generations of them. All over the house, miscellaneous colonies of bacteria. Spiders and flies, too, and moths and fleas all going about their business – all the minute, parallel lives this house accommodates.

He makes coffee, sits at the kitchen table and lights a cigarette. There are books and magazines strewn all over the table. A fly buzzes past his head, around the kitchen, then angles back to the dresser. Lily jumps on his lap, settles down and begins to purr. Her purrs vibrate in his thighs. He strokes her back, thinks of her little organs and entrails, the gestating foetuses. Her eyes grow drowsy. Sunlight streaming in the tall windows makes him drowsy too. His head is tender this morning; he shouldn't mix grape and grain. Lately he has started to visualise liver damage. The edges get frilly, tattered, discoloured, then the function slows. He is constantly looking for signs in himself – liver eyes, liver skin, pale stools. White specks on the fingernails, a nurse once told him, are the tell-tale signs doctors look for.

Lynch's dairy herd are fanned out on the front field beyond the lawn, empty udders swinging loosely. Bulls at the back

3

of the house, cows at the front – he is besieged by Lynch's beasts. Big Friesian cows, heads down grazing, filling up with milk again. Every morning they move in an eastwardly direction, then curve towards the south, like a great ship turning. Such a meek nature they have. He watches them intently. Not as melancholy as the cows of his childhood. Modern cows might be prone to interference from satellite signals or phone masts or the electronic bleeps and the spectral wavelengths of light-emitting diodes in the milking parlour, all this turbulence entering their consciousness and changing them, corrupting their nature, dulling their sensibilities. Poor, post-industrial cows. He watches them for a long time. The way they lift their tails and simultaneously defecate and urinate and masticate without as much as a how-do-you-do.

What to do today. He could cut away the furze and briars in the quarry, clear out the junk in the stables, rehang the doors. There's no shortage of work. Getting started is the problem. This solitary life is breeding in him a great immobility. Some days, sitting in the same position, he thinks he has been there for a few minutes when, in fact, hours have passed and suddenly it is noon or afternoon or four o'clock and the day outside has entirely changed.

He could go back to his teaching job in Belvedere. His happiest years, waking up in the little flat in Harold's Cross with Maeve beside him. Her warm breath and body. Sleepy sex before dawn, the smell and taste of her in his mouth, on his fingers. Standing under the hot shower, dazed, cleansed, then out into the cool morning air. His feet snug inside soft nubuck boots, bought in Clark's on Grafton Street. One hour it took to cross the city, south to north, down the Harold's Cross Road, into the little park just as it was opening at 8 a.m., out the other end, past the Hospice for the Dying. Thinking of the poor devils inside, gone to nothing, bones protruding under sheets, morphine pumps ticking away the pain. Unmerciful, he thinks now, not to allow mercy killing. He'd have done it himself to Josie if he could. Walking along, thinking of Maeve in the flat rising sleepily from the bed, showering, dressing, and then he'd be caught off guard by a crosswind coming up the canal on Harold's Cross Bridge. Below the bridge, Gordon's fuel yard, the coal and oil trucks lined up, ready for the day. On Clanbrassil Street a plaque on a wall for Leopold Bloom: citizen, husband, father, wanderer. *In the imagination was born . . .*

He puts two eggs on to boil. Husband, father, wanderer. Epithets all. *Citizen.* Who composes these inscriptions? Some arts officer in Dublin City Council who never as much as opened *Ulysses*. Confusing Bloom with the citizen! Husband, father, wanderer. What else? Dreamer. Schemer. Sinner. Humanist, feminist, pacifist.

The fly is back, zigzagging above Lucy's Irish dancing medals, coated with old grease and grime, on their velvet display. His own gold medal is in a velvet box upstairs. First in maths in the Leaving Cert in 1996. Dadda, in his gentleman farmer's tweed jacket and waistcoat, drove around the town on the tractor that evening, hooting the horn, a victory lap. First in the whole of Ireland. He was treated as special after that, marked out by destiny. Even before that, he had felt special. His father took him out of primary school on Friday afternoons, and they'd ride the tractor to the old folks' home up on the hill and dole out oranges and chocolate to the residents. How're you today, Teresa? Didn't Pat-Joe play well on Sunday, Dinny? He is, he's a great boy . . . *My son. In whom I am well* . . . On winter nights Luke and Lucy would lie on the drawing-room floor doing their homework, with Josie knitting by the fire and his mother below in the kitchen, smoking, alone with her thoughts, and his father would enter the room whistling, the smell of cold air off him, and he'd lean down and kiss each one of them on the head. He had come late to marriage and fatherhood. He must have pinched himself sometimes at his good fortune.

Poor Dadda. He never learned to drive the car. Less than a year after the victory lap, he suffered a sudden, fatal heart attack. No time for goodbye. Three days later Luke walked ahead of his funeral cortege up to the graveyard. He still remembers the sound of his footsteps on the road. Nothing else was audible — not the hum of the hearse's engine or the breeze in the trees. It had felt like a dream. The light of that May morning, the clear blue sky, the shimmering river. The stillness of everything. And then he flew, like it was the most natural thing in the world. He felt himself rise and hover above the road. Below him, the hearse and the mourners on foot and the cars coming slowly behind them. He could see it all: the road, the bridge, the avenue leading up to their house with no one home and all the rooms with all the furniture and beds and rugs awaiting their return. And the shiny black roof of the hearse glinting in the sun and the coffin inside and his father's body in a tweed suit and waistcoat supine on a bed of white satin, his beautiful face framed by a fringe of lace. He had never felt closer to him than at that moment. *Where are you taking me?* his father had asked. Up the road here for a rest, he replied. *Are you going to plant me?* I am. *Will I sprout?* You will, next spring. *Will I bloom?* You will, next summer. Luke felt the touch of his father's hand on his head ruffling his hair and he heard the beat of his own footsteps on the road again, the sound in tandem with the gentle waves lapping against the riverbank and the whistle of the reeds. And then a flock of little birds swooped down from above and flew on ahead and he heard their song – the authentic music of Eden – and he thought this is what it must feel like to walk into eternity.

A shaft of sun falls diagonally across the wooden table. He lights another cigarette. He had not been afraid that morning. He had felt his father's protection. The river, too, navigating him, something alive and benevolent – a little river sprite come to his aid in his hour of need, an imp of reason bringing order. The Imp of the Adverse. He peers at the grain of the wood in the table. The quantum properties of wood. Maybe he should have studied maths or science. A speck of cigarette ash drifts down in the air. He did not have the steam-power to be a mathematician, or a physicist. He frowns in concentration. What is it he is trying

7

to recover? Something that the ray of sun and the grain of the wood and the specks of ash are drawing out. With his index finger he presses an ash speck into the wood, then rubs the remaining ash between finger and thumb, over and back, until it is barely visible among the whorled contours of his fingertips. He stares at his thumb for a while. Strictly speaking, he might have been a little depressed last winter; the short days, the long nights, with only Ellen, his aunt who lives nearby, his regular company. But everything passes, and one evening in February he looked up from his book and saw the sun come through a gap in the trees and he sat in the same place the next evening and again the sun came through, and gradually the days lengthened and before he knew it, it was Easter.

He places two eggcups on a plate, pops the eggs in and pours a little salt on the side of the plate. Josie used to lick the salt off her plate. Her presence still throngs the house. He had to sell her hens at the market in Cork after she died; he couldn't bear the sight of them mooching around the yard, pining. Dirty auld things, his mother said, shitting all over the place.

At the table he pushes away some books to make room for the plate, then tops the eggs. Dadda used to top his and Lucy's eggs every morning. Something as trivial as topping an egg, no greater love. The yolk spills over and dribbles onto the plate. He adds a pinch of salt to each egg. With the edge of the spoon he shears albumen off the inside of the eggshell and mixes it with the soft yolk. In his mouth his tongue seeks out the solid texture of the albumen, suddenly repulsed by the thought of biting into the embryonic speckle in the yolk. He swallows hard, fearing queasiness. He rinses his palate with a mouthful of coffee and picks a book from the pile at the end of the table. *With Borges*. Borges's photo is on the front cover: a beautiful old man with tossed white hair gazing skywards. You'd never guess he was blind. Luke reads a few pages. Every night of his life Borges put on his long wool nightshirt and knelt down and recited the Our Father in English. He had ten names for the sky. He wrote something about angels too. Luke flicks through some pages. Not in this book.

He closes the book. There are books all over the house. He buys them in charity shops, second-hand bookshops, at auctions. Three for a euro, five for two euros. He collects magazines too — *New Scientist*, *Scientific American*, *Nature* — tempted by a headline: The Ultimate Quantum Paradox, Touching the Multiverse, Cosmic Coincidences, Four Radical Routes to a Theory of Everything, The Maths of Democracy, How Your Mind Warps Time, Why Darwin Was Wrong About the Tree of Life, Why Einstein Was Wrong About Relativity, The Strangest Liquid. Water, the multiverse, the Higgs Boson, the SpaceX project, fast radio bursts, the strangeness and charm of a quark — late at night he feasts on these articles, enthralled by every new finding, the moment amplified by the silence and the lateness of the hour and the intensity of his concentration, feeling alive to the multitudinous possibilities inherent in everything, feeling himself capable of understanding everything. In the small hours of the morning he often feels on the brink of a revelation or an illumination, close to the secret that unlocks some mystery of science and, if he fully attends, he will decipher it – if he focuses his whole being he will feel the vibrations of infinitesimal strings or come within a hair's breadth of deducing the quantum structure of time-space itself. And then the moment passes and the dawn arrives and he stands in his kitchen, flattened by the ludicrousness of these aspirations, these hallucinations.

The bookshelves are all full. There are books stacked in alcoves and recesses, on windowsills and side tables, on the return landing, in boxes under the back stairs. He has not read a quarter of them. He used to devour books, but these days, after reading just a few lines or a single page, he gets a kind of mental image of the whole book. *Books Read Even Before You Open Them Since They Belong to the Category of Books Read Before Being Written.* He remembers coming upon that line, the feeling of recognition it evoked. In his life there have been a few books that have left a lasting impression and on which he still sometimes dwells. Novels whose narrators experience certain moods and states of mind that he identifies with, and which are so subtle and delicate as to be almost impossible to describe. In those novels he found images and moods that he felt surprisingly connected to, and it is these connections that he hankers after. He can remember his exact surroundings and his state of mind when he read those novels, and those surroundings and those states of mind now seem inseparable from the characters and contents of the novels; there was no separation of worlds and the characters were as real and as stirring as if he and they were one, and they never afterwards left him.

Like Bloom, he thinks. No, Bloom is more. He is always close. As close as his own jugular vein. A second self. They are substrates of each other. Out of the same egg . . . Castor and Pollux. Divided natures too. Two dreamers, schemers, sinners. Space travellers. Transposers of souls. Transitioners of realms.

Moments like this he longs to be back in Belvedere. That morning walk, pigeons on the footpath, raucous gulls over-head. Buses pulling out from the kerb spluttering exhaust fumes on passing cyclists. All the lives parallel to his own, all the moments in which different things are simultaneously happening. Horizontal time. Thoughts and musings that seem to go on for hours, but take only minutes. No one understands time. Impossible to measure too. If it weren't for death, we might not count time at all . . . Under the arch at Christchurch, his watch reading 8.35, 8.36, 8.37 a.m. Vertical time. Downhill then and a whiff of the Liffey and a blast of wind, bracing on his face. More gulls screeching overhead on the north quays, the world their oyster. The world was his oyster then too. He had his life all mapped out – a few more years in the city, then he'd come back here with Maeve, work the land, fill the house with kids. Mammy, Josie, Ellen, the whole happy racket, like in the old days. Up Jervis Street, around Parnell Square and into Denmark Street as the Mercs and Beamers and Range Rovers pulled up, dropping off the uniformed sons of doctors, lawyers, judges. He was always moved by the way the big boys took their little brothers' hands and led them inside. He gets a lump in his throat thinking of them. Everything about the place . . . He felt close to Joyce there too. And Stephen. Thinking he *was* Stephen, leaning down to help some weak, misty-eyed boy. Moments when he felt himself simultaneously and symbiotically fused with the sweet boys before him and the image-memory of the young innocent Stephen Dedalus in those very rooms a hundred years before. Regularly going off script, off curriculum, spending weeks teaching nothing but *Ulysses*. Certain scenes: Stephen in class, Bloom with the cat and the kidney, the men in Hades going to bury the dead. Such mirth Luke had with his class, such wordplay and punning, the boys decoding, mapping it out, acting it out. Sir, sir, Leo Burke just ate with relish the inner organs of Beatty and Fowler. Shut your obstropolos, Carney! Sir, there's a tang of faintly scented urine off me sandwich. Oh ineluctable modality, oh jumping Jupiter! If he ever has a son he will send him to Belvedere or Clongowes. For all their faults, the Jesuits' ethos of care and service still prevails. Like Dadda, always setting example. No need to have any truck with the old boys' network.

He raises another spoonful of egg to his lips but feels the bile rising. He pushes his chair back, nerves jumping to attention in his thighs, and carries the plate to the front door. I do not like them, Sam-I-Am, I do not like green eggs and ham. A pack of half-feral cats swarm and pounce on the eggs. Greedy scuts. Lily, sleek-black and imperious, sits inside on the carpet. Haughty little madam, he thinks, and she from the same gene pool as this riff-raff. Generations of inbreds, Lily herself probably sired by her own father or brother. You wouldn't know it though, with her emerald eyes and shiny coat and perfectly proportioned body. Almost four now. He won't feel the years passing. I might have you stuffed, Lily, he says, put you up on the mantelpiece. He shudders. The eyes of the resurrected staring down at him.

His thoughts slip back to Belvedere again. He took a career break four years ago with the intention of doing something – writing a book perhaps – on Joyce or even Bloom. It was more than a whim, more than a money-making enterprise, though that too. It was an itch, a longing – a necessity even – to stay close to Bloom, to inhabit him day and night. But there was little he could add to the Joycean canon already in print and the endless supply of online material on Joyce. If he could draw or paint he might have attempted an illustrated guide to *Ulysses*. He thought about writing 'A Student Guide to Joyce' or '100 Factoids about Leopold Bloom' or '100 Fun Facts About James Joyce'. All too trivial. He wanted to do something of worth, something with heft. He tried to find some central organising principle. In the first year off work he read and re-read large sections of *Ulysses*, compiled lists of idioms, phrases and words – the singular, the colloquial, the vernacular. On his laptop he created files and folders and folders within folders into which he downloaded images of all sorts of Joyceanilia – a copy of Joyce's birth cert, Bloom's moustache cup, César Abin's question-mark portrait, photos of the Queens Hotel, Ennis – and wrote a paragraph of elucidation to accompany

13

each. From Ellmann's biography he lifted interesting anec-
dotes, titbits, witty excerpts from Joyce's letters to his father;
from Gifford's *Annotated Ulysses* he transcribed eleven items
related to Joyce's childhood homes; from Yale's Beinecke
library he downloaded a complete copy of Delmore
Schwartz's own heavily annotated *Finnegans Wake*. He wrote
a short essay about the awe he felt when he discovered that
Joyce's flesh and blood – in the body of Stephen Joyce –
still walked the earth. He wrote a profile of Bloom, then
one of Joyce, then a longer one of Bloom. The more material he compiled the more impossible the project became,
and the more dejected he grew. How to catch the peculiar
cast of Joyce's mind. How to convey what he felt for Bloom.
If he were a novelist he might have been up to the task. He
had been greatly taken by a character in a novel who herself
had written a novel called *The House on Eccles Street*, in which
Marion Bloom refuses to have sex with her husband until
he works out who he is. Luke would have read this novel,
if it had existed.

One by one the cats drift off and he is left. He feels the
strangeness of standing in the doorway. He steps out into
the sunlight, warm granite under his bare feet, the sun's heat
penetrating bone and marrow. He gazes out over the lawn.
In the field beyond, the cows are lying down, full now,
chewing the cud. Full with the view too: the sloping fields
and hedgerows, the river, everything radiating out from the
house towards the river. From the corner of his eye, something moves. A magpie lands on the blue bloom of a
hydrangea with something in its beak. A mouthful of old

cork – wine cork. No. A turd. Short and thick and dry, stale enough to hold together. A cat turd. He never knew birds ate old shit. Pigs eat each other. He looks down the avenue as words trail across his mind. Coprophagia. Pica. Anorexia. Schizophrenic hunger.

MID-MORNING, HE IS stirred from reverie by the sound of an engine coming up the avenue. Jim Lynch's jeep passes the window into the yard. Luke waits for the sound of his footsteps, the knock on the back door.

'Come in, come in, Jim.' He stands at the end of the table. 'Sit down.'

Jim Lynch removes his hat, sits down, places the hat on his right knee. He is coming earlier and earlier each year, sensing some change.

'Wasn't that some wedding beyond in the castle at the weekend, Jim? Ha?'

'Ay, an oligarch's daughter, by all accounts,' Lynch says. He taps the hat uneasily.

'A million euros, I believe, just to hire the place for the week. Imagine! The Duke is fairly creaming it.'

'He is, all right.' Lynch narrows his eyes. His colour is high, like Dadda's when he got anxious. He needs to watch that. Nearly a goner last year; had to be pulled out of

17

the slurry tank by one of the sons. Must have slipped.

'Jesus, Jim, no one knew what an oligarch was until a few years ago.'

Lynch nods.

'And d'you remember the big bash that footballer had for his twenty-first last year?'

Another nod.

'Premier league lad, what's this his name is?'

Lynch shakes his head, impatient to move on.

'They rent out the whole place, living quarters and all. Who'd have thought it, Jim, the commoners traipsing in and out of the Duke's private quarters?'

'It's a turnaround, all right . . . Still, I suppose they bring a bit of business to the area, a few jobs.'

Fuck-all business they bring, Luke wants to say, with their big transport trucks coming over on the ferry to Rosslare, laden with everything from bottled water to truffles. Even bring their own chefs and barmen.

Lynch transfers his hat to the other knee. 'How's Ellen keeping? I haven't seen her out for a while.'

His father's sister, his maiden aunt. After a lifetime in America she retired to her bungalow on the hill where, from his own bedroom window every night, he can see the lights of her bedroom and knows if she's gone to sleep. 'She's good. I call up to her every day. And we take the odd trip to Cork or Waterford for a bit of shopping or for a hospital appointment.'

Lynch nods. He runs a hand over his thin greasy strands of hair, then rubs his stubble. Itching to get down to business.

'The bulls are thriving,' Luke says, after a few moments.

'They are,' Lynch replies, a note of irritation in his voice.

'They do fair leppin' these nights in the full moon. Fair churning up of the ground too.'

'Is that so?'

Lynch is trying to play a cool game. With his large dairy herd he needs Luke's land to supplement his own farm. He knows Luke could easily re-let it in the morning for top dollar, leaving him in the lurch.

'Apparently it's common for bulls to go mad in a full moon – there was a piece in the *Farmers' Journal* about it a few weeks back.'

'Is that right?'

Luke turns to the window. 'The milkers are looking great out there too,' he says, signalling at the cows. 'There's what – eighty there now?'

There are one hundred and eight cows grazing in the field.

Lynch nods. He knows well Luke has counted them.

'Ye must have a fine yield, with the growth we're having this summer. Jesus, I'd nearly eat that grass myself!' Lay it on, thick and fast. 'And the bulls,' he adds, 'they'll definitely be U's or even E's when they kill out.' Big fat profit for you, Jim Lynch, he wants to say. Better not overdo it. Not right, either, scoring points at the expense of the poor beasts. They'll be going to the factory soon enough. That time years ago he and Dadda brought a load of heifers to the Kepak factory – the halal place – and nothing would do Dadda but to go up the line. The Muslim guy in bloodied

19

garb saying the blessing over each animal as he slit their throats. *Allahu Akbar.* Other prayers too, whispered in the ear. Thanking Allah . . . The way the heifers walked obediently down the gangway that day. The eyes of a human the last thing they saw.

'Tis, tis good, all right. Of course we spread urea and nitrogen every spring – and slurry – so it's well looked after.'

'Great. I must take a soil sample one of these days.' Keep him on his toes! He'd love nothing better than if I were clueless, but I'll tickle his catastrophe, believe you me! 'You know they reckon there's only about sixty years' worth of soil left in the world. With all the intensive farming – and with the loss of the rain forests and erosion and everything – we're running out of soil.' He shakes his head. 'Sixty harvests, Jim . . . imagine that.'

The cat walks in and is about to jump up on the table when she sees Lynch and freezes. He throws her a look. Probably afraid of cats. A bad sign in a man. Probably held squirming sacks under water, waiting for the bubble-bubble. No prayer there to send them on their way.

'Come on, Lily. Up!' Luke leans down and sweeps the cat onto his lap in one swift, fluid movement. Lynch will think him a sissy. Who cares? They have him down as eccentric around here anyway with all the cats and the house full of books.

Lynch straightens up. 'Brian and myself are drawing up a five-year plan for the farm. I'll be sixty soon, so . . . Brian wants to phase out the Friesians and get into Holsteins instead.'

Brian Lynch, tall, handsome, brown-eyed, only two years younger than Luke. The other brother Kevin must be twenty-eight now. Always fond of Brian. He spent a year on an intensive dairy farm in New Zealand a few years back. A massive place, five thousand acres, he told Luke. Lived with the family, treated him like a son. Run off their feet, as many as twenty newborns every morning in the calving season. They kept the little heifer calves for breeding, got rid of the bulls. One morning there were twelve new arrivals – five heifers and seven bulls. The farmer handed Brian the humane killer and told him to go into the shed and shoot the seven little bulls. 'And did you?' Luke asked. 'Did I fuck! I turned on my heel and walked away and he went in and shot them himself.'

'We had a fellow out from Teagasc the other day,' Lynch continues, 'advising us about things. Anyway, the long and the short of it is I might take a five-year lease from you.' He pauses, looks Luke in the eye. 'I can give you two years up front.'

Five years, Luke thinks, you will in your hole! Trying to inveigle your way in here like that! Too long in situ, getting too comfortable, that's the trouble.

Jim Lynch did Luke a favour by leasing the land when his father died, thus sparing Luke from returning from university in Dublin. In the early years Lynch did as he pleased – knocked gaps in ditches, put up gates, acted like he owned the place. He covets the farm. They all do. Finest land on the Sullane – they'd all give their eyeteeth to have this road and river frontage. Fishing rights too – the right to hunt, hawk, fish and fowl. Deed and title taken up by Luke's grandfather and namesake Luke Carthage O'Brien in 1921. All the papers are in the filing cabinet in the study.

'Five, bedad,' Luke says, with a bemused chuckle, which sounds phoney. He is not cut out for this lark.

'With two years' rent up front.'

Luke had heard it the first time and his heart had jumped. He could do with the money. If he doesn't return to teaching he will have to take the land back and farm it himself. It's the only solution. Even without livestock, he'd be eligible for several EU grants. In addition, he could sell three or four cuts of silage a year, and, with the forestry grant he gets for the oak trees, he would get by. And the shame of another man – a neighbour – living off the fat of his land would be eliminated. But it would mean, too, forfeiting city life for ever.

'Ah, sure we'll stick with the yearly lease, Jim,' he says. He places a hand under the cat and gently lifts her to the floor. 'I'll be taking it back next year anyway, or the year after at the latest.'

The blood flares bright on Jim Lynch's cheeks. He won't find another place to rent as convenient as this. He bites his lower lip, livid. Thinking Luke a pup now, a brat. He wants a farm for each son and expects, no doubt, that some day soon he'll buy Luke out. Well, not if I have to sell the clothes off my back, Luke thinks, will I ever sell an acre of Ardboe.

'I can give you three years up front, if you like,' Lynch says then.

Luke drops his hand by the side of his chair, spreads his fingers wide. He had to go to Lynch once for an advance. It was after he had come back to mind Josie. Lynch doesn't have to look further than Luke's banger of a car outside or the chipped paint on the front door to know that money is short.

'Ah, we'll stick with the arrangement we have, Jim. It has served us well enough this far.'

Luke rises. Lynch, taken by surprise, rises too, his hat almost falling off his knee.

'I'll do out the lease in September, as usual,' Luke says.

There will be hell to pay now for the rest of the summer – tractors revving and roaring up and down the fields around the house. And in the winter, heavy machinery churning up the ground.

Luke watches the jeep roll past the window. He is struck at the sad figure Lynch cuts as he drives away, staring straight ahead, the hat on his head, his broad shoulders and back. He is not the same at all since that fall into the slurry pit. Shook-looking, a haunted look in his eyes. Luke wonders if he saw something. He had the same thought the first time he saw photos of Seamus Heaney in public after his stroke. A changed man, as if he had returned from somewhere.

He paces back and forth on the kitchen floor, addled. Maura Lynch laid out Josie upstairs in her room. The two families were always close. Jim is getting old. What is he doing, after all, except trying to do the best for his family? You can't fault a man for that.

THE CHURCH BELLS are ringing out the Angelus when he pulls the front door behind him and starts down the avenue. He hates this time of day, the lethargy, the ennui. Six minutes and about a thousand steps, he once calculated, to get to the end of the avenue, though he has never succeeded in counting past two hundred. He should keep a log: record the dates, times, weather conditions, prevailing winds. Ascertain to what degree the time of day and weather conditions affect his speed. Other variables too: type of footwear and clothing worn, state of mind, proximity to sleep, proximity to the consumption of solids and liquids, to intoxicants, to music, sex, literature. He smiles at the thought. Determine the extent, if any, philosophy or poetry or porn affects pedestrian speed.

Lily is beside him, her tail held high and straight. She trots off ahead. He coughs hard, spits out sputum. His throat is dry and sore; he has a touch of heartburn too. Pregnant women get heartburn — caused, his mother used to say, by the hair on the child's head tickling the mother's chest. Certain smells sicken them – coffee, fried bacon. It's worse for some. Maeve didn't get that far along. The child would be eight years old now. His child. He or she. More males miscarry – the universe is hard on males, in utero, ex utero. We die younger, more suicides too. Up ahead, Lily is stopped at a tree, her backside to the trunk. *Pssss-pssss*, Luke teases. *Mingo Lily.* She turns her head away indignantly. Wonder if animals miscarry. Why wouldn't they? Chromosomal abnormalities in every species. A misbirth with trailing navelcord. Stephen Dedalus, watching the midwife with her bag of tricks coming down the steps onto Sandymount Strand. Mrs Florence McCabe, relict of the late Patrick. Or relic, which is it? Rarely used now. Should've put 'relic of Denis' in Mammy's death notice. What had she in the bag? Navelcord. Eve had no navel, a belly without blemish. *Gaze in your omphalos.* Always love that word omphalos, the sound of it. Wells and pumps and turloughs, hatches into the underworld. Gaze into the astral soul of man.

He turns and looks at the house, walking backwards for a few steps, the sun warm on his back. Such love he feels for this place, for the regular and ceaseless procession of the seasons, watching the growth in trees and plants and fields recede after each summer, recover after each winter. He squints, then closes one eye, testing his vision. The whole house looks neglected. Doors and windows not painted in twenty years. He bought ten litres of white gloss in the spring. New paint brushes, white spirit, masking tape. He only got as far as cleaning and sanding three windows.

Nothing to stop him resuming, he thinks. Can start when he gets back. One door a day: wash, sand, undercoat, then two coats of paint. After that, a window a day. He makes the calculation. If he works six days a week he'll be done by the beginning of September.

His gaze settles on the round windows in the east wing above the kitchen. These four portholes, which pour light into the loft, have always baffled him. Why, twelve miles inland from the sea, did a nineteenth-century architect insert four ship's windows into the design of a Georgian house? He turns ninety degrees to the left, in the direction of the river and the light reflecting up from the water. Constant river traffic in those days, boats and barges coming up on the tide with supplies for the town. The architect acknowledging the river's presence, he thinks. More to it than that, something more deliberate and specific. His eyes linger on the portholes, mulling their enigma. Clearly visible to passing vessels. He imagines a head appearing at one of the portholes . . . a woman's face. The lady of the house, standing there by prior arrangement maybe. A love sailing away, forbidden love — the architect himself — leaving, and this the last glimpse. *Remember me always.*

Go home, Lily! He chases the cat back up to the house. Little madam, venturing this far down the avenue. If anything ever happened to her . . . Above, a fly-past of swallows, or starlings — he can never tell the difference. He watches them for a few moments. No high jinks, no murmurations this time of year. Rounding the last bend on the avenue he steps onto the grass verge and walks between two rows of the

27

oak plantation he planted six years ago. One morning a few months after Josie's death, four words arrived to him out of sleep: *twelve thousand oak saplings*. Memorial of Josie. Sequesters of carbon. His mother said nothing when he told her his plan. Thinking, What'll you plant for me?

Nervously, his eyes scan the tree trunks. He's barely able to look. He moves along the row. No sign of canker, no oozing. He examines the leaf tips. No dieback. He moves from row to row, going deeper into the plantation. He has avoided checking them for weeks. Fourteen thousand oaks were felled in Guagán Barra last month. He could lose the entire twelve thousand. *Phytophthora ramorum* is general all over Ireland, one of several plagues arriving from the east. Dutch elm, sudden oak, beech wilt, sweet chestnut blight. Bleeding canker. He can see the future – the end of wood-lined roads, parks, riverbanks, towns no longer sheltered by ash.

He walks on. Trees calm his naked nerves. The sight of a tree, especially in winter, bare against the sky, beautiful. He stands and strokes a trunk. So young and tender and innocent. It's easy to be innocent when you're a tree. Maybe he should say a prayer for them. Make a deal with God: Spare my oaks and I'll cover this land with trees. Trees will be my legacy, like the great oak and beech stands on the Duke's estate three miles away. A few hundred years from now, someone will stand here before gnarled trees and huge crooked roots and discern something of these times, of this family. That German forester who wrote about the hidden life of trees, how they are bound together in families, communicating through a web of underground fungi. Mycelium. Sending warning signals when danger approaches, feeding the weak with nutrients. He squats down, listening. Around him, the trees are alert, leaves talking, roots entwining, branches bowing down in grief for lost loved ones.

As he makes his way out of the plantation he is gripped by a spasm of pain. The pain is behind, in the vicinity of his kidneys. He rubs his back. If he dropped dead now, he might not be found for days. No one would miss him. After a day or two of not hearing from him Ellen would be worried and walk up to the house and let herself in, and, finding the remains of his breakfast on the table and the scavenging cats, she would raise the alarm.

At the end of the avenue he turns left and walks along the road towards the town. To his right the glitter of water, familiar, beautiful, unknown too. You get used to beauty, he thinks, you grow immune, you devour it with greedy eyes. On the other side of the stone wall, little black and white, thin-legged birds hop along the riverbank, turning their heads jerkily to the right and left. Some kind of tits or finches or wagtails. The luckiest of all creatures, birds. Escaped from reptilian existence eons ago to flit through sunlit meadows and rise into the heavens. Soul carriers in the running sky, translating nature's vibrations into song for human ears. No worries either, God will always provide. The way they fly down and befriend captive men, men in camps, men at the edge of reason.

He looks across the river to the Boathouse on the wharf,

and beside it, among the willows, eight architect-designed houses with exposed stone and glass walls and red cladding. Built during the boom five or six years ago and over-priced at the time, scarcely half of them are occupied now. Susceptible to gleam and glass and glossy brochures, he almost bought one as an investment. Up above the town, Clonduff House, partly concealed behind trees, nestles into the hill. From this perch the Blake family look down on the town and the surrounding countryside. If they deign to look at all, that is. Behind the house and the sloping lawn, the barns, stables, milking parlour, glasshouses and poly-tunnels are well hidden from the town. Unmarked trucks with their cargo of Clonduff Farm organic fruit and vege-tables come and go through the back gates of the estate, the fruit and veg destined for the shelves of Fortnum & Mason's and Harrods. Modelled on the Prince of Wales's enterprise in Cornwall, Luke thinks, though more discreet and with not as much as a nod to the townspeople below. Still, the Blake place is not a patch on Dunmore Castle and estate, the Duke of Berkshire's place three miles away. There are hierarchies everywhere and, compared to the Berkshires, the Blakes are only second-fiddle aristocrats. As a young man Luke's father and grandmother were invited for the pre-hunt hot toddies on the lawn of Clonduff House every St Stephen's Day – a nod, Luke supposes, to their almost castle-Catholic status. From up there, his father told him, there's a splendid view out over the town and surrounding countryside and Ardboe House – their house – below on the river plain, the closest of all the big houses in the valley.

A car drives out of the town along the Dunmore road, then slows and turns left onto the bridge. Luke salutes the driver, then walks on. As he enters the town, a huge SuperValu truck edges its way up Main Street between parked cars. A band of gulls passes over the rooftops, a long way from the sea at Errish now. Luke pauses on the footpath outside SuperValu and the glass doors slide open. A jeep turns into the yard of O'Donnell's Hardware and, as it disappears, the grey double doors of O'Grady's garage next door open and John O'Grady secures the bolt in the ground. There's no stir yet at either the Tavern Bar or the Sportsman's Inn across the street.

'Luke O'Brien, you should fuck off back to Dublin.'

Startled, he turns. Dilly Madden is beside him. Wild snow-white hair, pale face, red lipstick, red dress, pink beads – in full manic regalia today. She puts a hand on his arm. She must feel the hop in his nerves. Still, he welcomes this intrusion into his thoughts. This is my life now, he muses, when the yelp of a madwoman and the clasp of a mad-woman's hand are the most welcome things in my day. He has a soft spot for Dilly. She was his mother's only friend in her last years. Two brazen, broken, outspoken women. Drinking, throwing back their heads laughing. *Sans* decorum.

She is clacking her tongue now. 'What's keeping you here, Luke?' She sounds sane. Her voice is soft, concerned. 'In the name of God will you go back to Dublin, like a good lad. Sure there's nothing for you here.' The tiny lines of a smoker radiate out from her mouth. She's whiskery too. His mother was the same. Hormonal, more testosterone in some women, or something to do with the menopause maybe. Josie was the worst, always sprouting tough black hairs. 'Hairy baconface', Lucy called her. His cruel sister.

'I know, Dilly, I know. You're right.'

He wonders when she got out of St Declan's. She was sectioned in April – the daughter put her in. Sometimes she goes in of her own accord, taking Dillon's hackney into Waterford. In for the shelter, she says. She was inside when his mother died. He visited her a few weeks later, having a great need to talk to someone who knew and loved his mother. Dilly didn't want to hear about the funeral. She wanted only to talk about herself. She told him things that day that he wishes he never heard.

'Lock up that house, Luke, and go back to your teaching job. This bloody town'll kill you if you don't. I'm telling you, it'll eat you alive. Mark my words.' She had cancer a few years ago and wore a bad wig for a while. 'Above there in that big house on your own . . . A young man like you? It's not right! You should be living your life.'

He nods. Wonders if she remembers what she told him that day in Declan's.

'I will, Dilly, I'll go back at some stage. But . . . ah, you know yourself, I don't like leaving Ellen.'

'Don't mind Ellen. Ellen is grand, there's not a bother on Ellen. She has a nice warm house and a good pension. You can't be nursing old women all your life – you've done enough of that now.' She tut-tuts again. 'Where's that nice girl you used to bring down here before? Your mother thought a lot of her. Go back to her!'

Poor Dilly in Declan's day room that day, doped to the eyeballs. What do you do here all day, Dilly? He was only trying to make conversation. Do you read, Dilly? I'm not here to read, she said, I'm here to be mad. And then the talk came in torrents. She gave birth to a child when she was sixteen, fathered by her eldest brother, Michael. Michael Madden, respected town councillor, prosperous businessman, married for forty years with a grown-up family. Down the toilet it went with a plop, she said, I didn't know what was happening. She tapped her head with her index finger. There's a kink in every family, she whispered.

He touches her shoulder gently. 'I have to go, Dilly, I'm in a bit of a hurry.' He has to get away from her pained body.

He enters SuperValu and picks up a basket. Potatoes, carrots for the eyesight, McCloskey's granary bread. Comté cheese. Coke. He buys the same staples every time. A sirloin at the meat counter. From the fridge, Denny's hickory flavoured rashers, a half-pound of Denny's sausages . . . Always Denny's. Around a long time, 1904 at least. Leopold Bloom waiting at the butcher's counter and the next-door girl asking for a pound and a half of Denny's sausages. Bloom sneaking a look at her, fine pair of swinging hips on her. A bit mean of him, all the same, calling them hams. He puts his hand on a Clonakilty black pudding, then changes his mind. Cooked spicy pig's blood. He moves along the fridge to the chickens, naked under cellophane, open pores where feathers were plucked, fat breasts injected with God-knows-what to plump them up. Short painful life in cages. Never eats them any more. Joyce liked chicken. His eye doctor in Paris called to the flat one evening. Clothes strewn everywhere, the state of the place, and Joyce and Nora sitting on the floor, a pan with a chicken carcass between them, a half-empty bottle of wine beside them.

At the end of an aisle he casts a quick glance up ahead. Tea, coffee, breakfast cereals, Mrs Whelan, his old English teacher from St Mary's, now retired. He nods, smiles. 'Lovely day, Mrs Whelan.' It is indeed. He dawdles a bit, not wanting to be seen rushing to the wine. Aisle of flour, sugar, raisins, currants, sultanas, cornflour, Bird's Custard. Cowardy cowardy custard. The sight of the red, yellow and blue container brings a flash of nostalgia. Sunday dinner, Mammy, Dadda, Josie, Lucy and, every summer, Ellen home from America. As he reaches for a microwaveable carton it strikes him that, other than Ellen, Dilly Madden might be the last person in the town who cares about him. As he places the carton of custard into his basket he catches the sweet scent of vanilla. Lucy loved the scrapings of the saucepan: custard, rice, semolina, porridge. Let the bottom brown, Mammy. Laced with sugar, melty, silvery sheen. His mouth begins to water. He'll lob a spoon of ice cream into a bowl of hot custard later – delicious, the hot and cold sweet melt. Lucy is in Brisbane now. 28 Pear Street, Auchenflower. Came home alone for Mammy's funeral two years ago. Wonder if her kids have inherited her tastes and habits. Oliver and Ellie. Sunny days in the back garden – the back yard they call it, like the Yanks. Jim lighting the barbecue in the evenings. The pretty wooden house that Jim built. No, renovated. He built the deck and the barbie, even the cot when Oliver was born. Jim Mitchell, a carpenter from Banagh, fifteen years her senior. In a past era, it would have been regarded as an elopement. Jim must be nearly fifty now. He's ageing well, looking fit and tanned in photos. He doesn't have the smarts that Lucy has. Luke goes on Facebook some nights and peeks at their life, hits 'Like', and occasionally adds a comment. Oliver is seven; he looks a bit soft, a bit girly. Might be gay. It's obvious in some, there's no hiding it. Screamers, Oisín Kelly called them – they come out of their mothers screaming it.

He checks his watch. Brisbane is ten hours ahead. Lucy will be going to bed now. Or making the kids' lunches for school or laying things out for breakfast. No, tomorrow is Saturday. Winter there. He stops and reaches for a bottle of bleach, then changes his mind. Need to allow for the weight of wine. Rioja, or maybe a Barbera . . . *cúpla buidéal*, it being Friday. Or a nice crisp white maybe. An image of the evening ahead rises: sitting out on the lawn as the sun sets, sipping a dry white, chilled to perfection.

Outside, he leaves the bags down on the footpath and lights a cigarette. One of these winters, he'll visit Lucy. Christmas dinner on the beach. He hasn't been much of a brother – he should have gone out that time Ellie was ill. Febrile convulsions. Nearly lost her. Josie had epilepsy all her life. Wonder if Lucy admitted the fault line to the doctors. *The falling sickness.* The suggestible nature of certain words – he can feel the gravitational pull of those. Lear had it. *Tis very like he hath the falling sickness.* The sudden, frightening way that Josie used to fall forward. Once, while she was on the ground, Lucy chalked around her limp body. He remembered that when Ellie was sick. He was afraid something was coming home to roost for Lucy, some bad karma.

He throws away the cigarette butt. Too early to go home – the day is stretching out before him. He heads up the hill towards the square. The shopping bags are heavier than he expected. John O'Grady, sitting inside the garage window, looks up as he passes and Luke nods at him. He doubts if John is a trained mechanic at all; probably just fell into the family business. Never married, sits there in the window all day waiting for customers.

Suddenly he remembers: Caesar it was, not Lear, who had epilepsy. King George, too. Such a medieval-sounding ailment, consistent with a flat earth, Galileo, burnings at the stake. Haemophilia is like that too. The poor devils, thinking they had only one skin.

Up ahead John-Joe Cleary crosses the street, heading for the Sullane Valley Hotel for the €5 lunch. It used to be a fine place; had the meal there after Dadda's funeral. Now, the clientele is OAPs and bachelors. Wonder what's on the menu today. John-Joe was a good friend to Dadda always, helping out around the farm for years. He still helps out up at Blake's during the hunting season. Every now and again he goes on a bender. A quiet boozer, never a nuisance. Probably waiting for the mother to die and leave him the house. You'll never miss your mother till. Never saw him with a woman. Probably a bit afraid of women, thinks they're complicated. Keep life simple, get the €5 lunch every day. Before you know it, you're fifty. Wake up one day and you're sixty. Not long left then. An ease when it's all over.

Luke crosses the street, slows as he passes the hotel door and reads the chalkboard menu. Bacon and cabbage today. Inside, it's dark, with no sign of John-Joe. Too late now to enter, he thinks. Anyway he's not hungry. Wouldn't mind a chat with John-Joe though. Often has the impression John-Joe keeps something back, that he knows more about Luke than Luke himself knows. But Luke trusts him – John-Joe is faithful to his father's memory and to the family. Some residual sympathy still exists for the family, going back to the double tragedy in 1941 when his father's twelve-year-old sister, Una, fell down the well on New Year's Day and their father dropped dead in the yard six months later. Those who remember are dying out now, and the sympathy is waning.

The sun burns down on his head. He continues along Main Street, past Kealy's bar. His father was wearing a tweed waistcoat with a pocket-watch when he walked into Kealy's and first laid eyes on his mother on a summer's evening almost forty years ago. Who do you think you are, you and your waistcoat? she thought, as she pulled his pint. Fifteen years her senior and countless stations above her, he was instantly smitten. She'd been a barmaid in Coventry, escaping, for a few years, the drunken father and cowed mother and the two-roomed cottage full of kids on the side of Croghan mountain. He spent a long time courting her, convincing her. The waistcoat still hangs in the wardrobe, its girth too great for Luke.

He crosses the street to the shade and sits on the windowsill of a boarded-up terraced house. Half the houses and shops in the town are boarded up. The feeling of decay and dereliction always in the air. Stagnancy. Listlessness in the young men – nothing to do, no work – hanging around the town. He feels a little light-headed. He reaches into one of the bags and brings out the bottle of Coke and takes a few slugs. The street is deserted. At the top of the hill, teachers' cars are parked in a line in the lay-by outside the primary school. Inside, he pictures little heads bent over desks. Not long now before the summer holidays.

He heads out the Dunmore road. He does not want to go home. He remembers the can of gloss paint waiting in the basement. He turns left onto the bridge, leaves down his bags and leans on the wall. Below him, the glimmer of water, the play of sunlight and wind and trees and sky on the surface, the currents and underwater motion almost invisible. Reeds, green and nervy, rise from the shallows. He turns his head. Half a mile downriver, the concrete bunker of the abandoned chicken factory is just visible beyond the trees. Decades' worth of chicks hatched out at one end. Birth to death in a hundred yards. Other dark goings-on there too for years. Poor boys from the terraces desperate for summer jobs and Vinnie Molloy, supervisor, pervert, brute, had the giving of the jobs. For certain favours rendered. Conor Mahon. Sean Byron. Kevin Kelly. Trying not to cry out with the pain. Always the poor who get raped.

He leans over the top of the bridge and searches for his reflection in the water. The shadow of a drowned man is supposed to be waiting for him in the water. Conor Mahon's shadow waiting for him here when he was twenty-one. Luke sat beside Conor in first year in secondary school, the two of them full of devilment. That day the priest came in to give a sex education lesson. Take these little bookeens home with ye, lads, he said. He returned the next day. Well, Conor, did you read the book? Oh I did, Father, I did . . . and 'twas the dirtiest book I ever read. Conor used to play the banjo. Started a band with three young ones when he was sixteen – Three Birds and a Badger, he called it. Luke cornered Molloy one night after Conor's death, threatened to cut off his fingers and toes if he ever touched another lad in the town. You'll be fucken walking on your heels, you scumbag, you'll have to be fed through a tube. Molloy hanged himself the week before his trial.

Luke straightens up. There has always been a pall over the town, he thinks, something dark and blighting, the cause of which he cannot put his finger on. Even during the economic boom, the air of depression and neglect never lifted. Old usurper's shadow still hanging over the valley. Imperialist thieves. Sir Richard, like his Blake forefathers, still collecting ground rent from businesses in the town but never giving back a penny to plant a tree or put a lick of paint on the terraces or a bench in the square. Take, take, take. A wave of anger flares in him.

He draws his gaze back to the flow of water rounding the bend in the river. He remembers the day in third class when Miss Fahy ran her wooden pointer along the line of a river on the physical map of Ireland. When the river suddenly changed direction Luke made the connection and transposed in his mind the river on the map to the river at the end of the town, and suddenly the penny dropped and it dawned on him that this was their river, and their bend and their land – O'Brien land – and it was up there on the map of Ireland for the whole class and the whole world to see. It was the first surge of familial pride that was woken in him. Here, at the little peninsula they call the Inch at the very edge of his land, the Sullane swings suddenly to the south, a ninety-degree rotation executed millions of years ago. Before it was named, before this place was touched by humans, the river captured the drainage system of another lower, lesser river and met a strange new tide coming up from the sea. A pirate then, the Sullane, Luke thinks now, a bully and a thief, usurping the route and riverbed of another. He had never thought of it like that before.

A plastic Coke bottle comes floating under the bridge. A sudden flash of anger at litterlouts, at the wanton thoughtlessness of someone just tossing their rubbish over their shoulder. Wanton thoughtlessness everywhere in evidence. Human stupidity too. Road rage, fish kills, farm effluent, phone masts, mindless government policies, or lack thereof. He keeps his eyes on the plastic bottle, tracking it for twenty or thirty yards. It flows out and around the tip of the Inch, appearing smaller and smaller as it floats off downriver, the sun still glinting on the plastic. Tossing on the waves all the way to Errish where the river enters the sea, where fresh water meets salt and swirls in little eddies, the salt nosing underneath, the fresh floating on top, no mixing or melding, no fusion of molecules.

He walks along the road and turns in the avenue. He can always feel when the afternoon changes and evening falls. Something in his circadian clock, he thinks, the way hibernating animals sense when the light fades.

The house has settled around him, restive now. He opens a bottle of Rioja, admires the ruby glow of the wine streaming into the glass. He sips it, lets it linger on his palate for a moment, then down his gullet it goes. Outside, a bird is singing in short sweet trills. Maeve had wanted to get a parrot for the flat in Harold's Cross but he never liked the idea of caged birds. Joyce kept two little parakeets for a while in Paris, Pierre and Pipi. One of them flew in the window one day and stayed and, not wanting it to be alone, he acquired the other. Probably saw it as a sign. Wonder if he clipped their wings. Or taught them to speak. Or sang to them. Probably spent hours peering at them with his poor eyesight, delighting in their plumage, in their little nipping and kissing and beak tapping. Leaning in closer, imitating their whistles and chirrups, picking up their secret little tones in his inner ear . . . slipping deeper and deeper into communion with them until he emitted his own little trills and twitterings in reply to theirs. Luke remembers buying a book about birdsong; it's somewhere in the house. Every morning at dawn the author entered an aviary in a zoo – in Philadelphia or Pittsburg – and played his flute to the birds. As time passed the birds started to imitate his notes and sing back to him.

He boils potatoes, fries the steak in a little butter and garlic, then lifts it onto a warm plate and lets the brownish meat juice trickle over it. Lily will soon appear, drawn by the aroma. At the table he draws the Borges book and a book of Derek Mahon's poems close to him. Certain nights are right for poems and he has a knack of opening a page at random, hitting on exactly the right one. He pours more wine. When he cuts into the steak, blood-brown juices run out, and he salivates. The meat is delicious. He thinks of Bloom's pork kidney and wonders why he ate pork. He wonders if it really is possible to taste urine off a cooked kidney. He remembers his alarm the first time he got a strong sulphurous whiff off his own urine after eating asparagus.

He eats another forkful of steak, then some potato sopping in juice. The potato melts in his mouth. Another forkful of steak. The eyes of this cow will pursue me through all eternity. Poor Bloom. The weight of feeling he carried on his shoulders. Such humanity. Joyce too, a gentle soul. His whole life marred by illness and poverty and Lucia's madness. Only fifty-eight when he died. Perforated ulcer. Luke was shocked when he came upon the post-mortem report as a footnote in Ellmann's biography. Reading it felt like rummaging through the body itself. Paralytic ileus. Extensive bleeding. Enormously dilated loops of small bowel as large as a thigh, coloured purple. *Head section not permitted.* His stomach must have been cut to ribbons from all the white wine. If only he'd listened to Nora and gone to a doctor, instead of paying heed to the Jolases and the other intellectuals telling him for years that the stomach pains were psychosomatic. All that genius . . . gone for ever. Feel him close still. Always. Have to keep the Ellmann book close to hand. He had a blood transfusion the day before he died and received the blood of two Swiss soldiers from Neuchâtel. A good omen, he thought, because he liked Neuchâtel wine. His last hours. Slipping into a coma. Waking in the night, asking for Nora. His coffin carried up the hill through the snow to the Fluntern cemetery. Eternally with me.

He must not exhaust himself thinking. Random inchoate thoughts following on more random inchoate thoughts. *Thought is the thought of thought.* The pressure of thoughts some-times, ideas turning cartwheels in his mind. Coming in surges, fast-flowing, flooding. *All is in all.* His speech too, at times. His father always at him. 'Easy, Luke, easy, slow down.' In class in Belvedere he'd stray off-topic, once extolling the beauty and harmony and symmetry in nature's fabric that is everywhere discernible – in the nucleus of a nut or an atom – and the boys saying, 'Slow down, sir, you're going too fast.' Maeve too. 'Stop! What are you talking about? Luke, you're making no sense!' He couldn't understand why she couldn't keep up. Moments like that, he had felt alien-ated. One night, she stopped him mid-stream. 'I bet you're bipolar,' she said quietly, nodding slowly. 'You're just like my uncle Mattie.'

He sips more wine. Bipolar. A touch, maybe. Occasional

highs, definite lows. Restlessness. Some hubris. Nothing delusional – his own mind does not mislead him. Certainly nothing that warrants intervention. They dope you to the gills. Like a veil thrown over everything. All you'd miss.

Lulled and sated, he picks up the Mahon book, opens page 81. *Let them not forget us, the weak souls among the asphodels.* Asphodel meadows, where the souls of those who did neither good nor bad reside. He looked up the asphodel flower once and when he clicked on the images and recognised the yellow flowers – which he had always assumed were a variety of iris – as identical to the flowers that appear every summer at the edge of the Inch, he was momentarily floored. Mythical flowers from Hades growing here on his land, right under his nose. What were the chances!

Irises were Maeve's favourite flowers. He brought her home a bunch of blue ones to celebrate the good tidings of great joy. Two weeks later it was all over and when they came home from the hospital she lay on the bed facing the wall. He lay beside her, then stood at the window. Nothing to say. Above, the night sky, the stars, the indifferent earth. A mistake of nature. Unplanned anyway. Better to happen now than at age four or fourteen, he told her later. They got hammered the following weekend and fell in the door at 3 a.m., and onto the bed, laughing. To think it was all over. A heavy period, that's all it amounted to, blood clots flushed down the toilet. A life, a life not . . . No soul yet. Or was there? Forty days before ensoulment occurs, the Greeks believed. Islam says one hundred and twenty. The yogis say it happens at the moment of conception when the ovum meets the sperm. A flash of astral light, then the soul rushes in. Wonder if a couple's spiritual goodness and wholesomeness matters, if their devotion to each other helps serve as a divine magnet to draw a good soul towards them. Wonder where the soul resides. Not in the body or blood, it being metaphysical, not physical . . . All those years in the grave, the blood of those two soldiers mixed with Joyce's and settled in his body. Traces still there maybe. One body, three bloods. A trinity of blood, he'd have liked that! Wonder what the soldiers were doing in the hospital that day.

He reads the poem. *A thousand mushrooms crowd to a keyhole.* He leaves his head in his hands. Tired. Foresees the road ahead, the years ahead . . . Sleepy . . . Shouldn't sleep here . . . He can do whatever he wants. He lifts his head and smiles. If you behave, Borges said to his six-year-old nephew, I will give you permission to think of a bear. I will give you permission to think . . . A thousand souls crowding to a door, waiting to be born . . . crying *Me, Me* . . . Go back, go back, it's not your turn yet.

FROM THE KITCHEN window he watches a red van snaking up the avenue. As it passes the window the driver turns his head and meets Luke's eyes before continuing on into the yard. Casing the joint. It happens about once a week – they see the big house from the road and take a chance.

He stands at the front door and puts out his hand when the van approaches from the yard. The passenger lowers his window and Luke leans in.

'Morning, lads,' he says, throwing his eyes over the driver and passenger. 'Ye're out early.'

'How's it going, boss?' the driver replies. A big, burly, red-faced fellow with ash-blond hair. A slightly younger version of the same man sits in the passenger seat.

'What can I do for ye?'

'Would you have any auld scrap lying around? Any auld iron or copper?'

'Devil the bit,' Luke says. He keeps his eyes hard on the

driver, then makes a big show of looking into the back of the van. Plastic bags, lengths of rusty iron, a marble fireplace. 'Ye're not local, are ye? I haven't seen ye around here before.'

'Ah, not far, boss – the far side of Mallow. What about new windows?' He nods towards the house. 'This man here can get the best of PVC windows for you.'

'No, no, ye're grand. I'm not interested.' He slaps the roof of the van twice, takes a step back. 'All right, so . . . Good luck, now.' Off with ye and don't come back, he wants to add.

He waits until the van is out of sight at the end of the avenue, then sits on the step. He needs to put up gates at the entrance and proper mortice locks on the front and back doors. He'll come home some day to find the place cleaned out. One kick to the back door and they're in. The Adam fireplace, the furniture, Dadda's gold pocket-watch, Ellen's trunks. A small fortune sitting in there.

The granite step is warm. It was on this step his mother was felled two years ago. A beautiful day in June. Sitting here talking away to him while he planted annuals in the flowerbed beside the front door. She had had him all to herself for several years. No more Josie, no more aggro. He had begun to enjoy her too – her fierce wit, her ferocious tongue.

'Get me an ice cream,' she ordered. He tipped a little plant out of its pot and set it in the soil, then turned to look at her. Her eyes were closed, her face tilted upwards towards the sun. He stood and looked out over the fields and down across the river to the town. A perfect day, he thought. He went inside and brought her out a choc-ice and bent again to the flowerbed, his back to her. A little puff of wind blew the ice cream wrapper past him, and he reached out his hand to try and catch it. It came to rest against a pot. Stay, he urged it. But another little gust blew it on; it stopped and started and worried along for a few more feet. He stood up and went after it.

'You're a rip!' he said, waving the wrapper as he returned. 'Why do you always have to make work for me?' His role now was the exasperated parent to her naughty child. It was the way she loved too – with robust gesture and combat. He resumed the planting and waited for her mocking jibe.

But none came, and he prodded again. 'Here I am, morning, noon and night, serving you . . . Jesus, and you haven't an ounce of gratitude or consideration for me – or for anyone! Do you know that?'

Again, no response. He turned to look at her. On her face, a wry crooked smile, a fixed grin.

'What?' he asked. The grin remained, lending her a look of stupidity. Mimicking Josie, he thought. I have a thundering bitch for a mother. 'Stop that,' he said and turned back to the work. Again he waited for the quip, the wisecrack reply. Again, none came. He turned around. The same frozen grin.

'Stop messing, Mammy . . . For fuck's sake . . . Stop it, it's not funny.'

Her face was tilted, her left eye half closed. The choc-ice slipped from her fingers onto the step. Mammy, he said urgently, jumping up. From her twisted mouth came a guttural sound. Her head slumped to one side. He leaned towards her and touched her face, then lifted her left arm. It fell, slack. His stomach lurched. He took out his phone and dialled. He kept saying her name. 'It's okay, you'll be all right.'

He lays his hand on the warm granite. On this stone a cataclysmic neurological event occurred in his mother's brain. He rubs the granite. We know not the day nor the hour, nor the stone. He wonders if she had a premonition. After four weeks in hospital she recovered sufficiently to be moved to rehab. Then, in the ambulance en route there, she was struck by a greater and, this time, fatal cerebrovascular event.

Just after eleven, another vehicle – a small yellow car – comes up the avenue. Again he goes to the front door. The car stops and a girl steps out. Small, striking-looking with very pale skin and short, jet-black hair. She nods and half turns to close the car door. Then she stands before him and meets his gaze calmly. She is thirty, perhaps thirty-two. Not a girl, but a woman.

'Hello,' she says, smiling. She glances at Lily, standing in the doorway behind him.

'Hello,' he says.

Lynch's Friesians are grazing in the field behind her. Just as she puts one foot in front of the other in a forward motion to offer her hand, a cow moves gracefully behind her head, from right ear to left, oblivious in her grazing to the beautiful simplicity in the motion of cow and girl.

She introduces herself, Ruth Mulvey, and he does likewise.

'I'm sorry for barging in on you like this,' she says. 'They told me in SuperValu that you might want a dog. I was going to put up a notice and the woman at the till said you might be interested. Katie, her name was.' Then, a little bashfully, 'She said to say she sent me.'

She gestures towards the car. 'It's my uncle's dog. He's gone into a nursing home. I have to go back to Dublin and I can't take him with me.'

Luke peers into the car. A small brown dog is curled on a blanket on the back seat. Without lifting its head, its eyes fix anxiously on Luke. Katie Cullen works part-time in SuperValu, and has the same bleeding heart for animals as he has. She comes up and feeds his cats whenever he goes away. The size of your place, she says, if I had it, I'd have fifty dogs.

The girl looks to Luke before opening the back door of the car.

'Go on, sure take him out,' he says, with a nod.

She lifts out the dog, its ears flattened, its body trembling in her arms.

'This is Paddy,' she says. She grips him tighter to mask the trembling.

'Paddy,' Luke repeats. 'How are you, Paddy!'

She raises her face to his and when their eyes meet her mouth widens into a broad smile, and he smiles back, elated.

They are standing very close. She comes up only to his shoulders. He can see the top of her head, the line of scalp where her hair is parted. He had forgotten how good it feels to be this physically close to a woman.

51

'Bring him into the house,' he says and turns and leads the way.

She sets the dog down on the rug in the drawing room. Rigid, tense, wary, the dog doesn't move and they stand staring at him.

'The poor devil,' Luke says softly, then turns to her. She has long dark eyelashes. Green eyes. Beautiful. Something a little funky about her – her hairstyle maybe. 'Sit down,' he tells her. 'I'll get him a bit of meat or something. Will you have something yourself – tea, coffee?'

'No thanks, I'm grand. And don't worry about Paddy – he's probably too anxious to eat. He's had a lot of change lately and I think he's sensing there's more to come.'

He goes down to the kitchen and runs the cold tap and fills two glasses of water. When he returns, the dog is crawling on its belly towards her feet.

She is from Curraboy, three miles away.

'Only out the road,' he says. 'I don't think we've ever met before, have we?'

She shakes her head. 'I don't think so. Although we may well have, at some stage, around the town. At football matches maybe.' Then she gives a little laugh. 'Or Irish dancing years ago – everyone meets at Irish dancing!'

'Did you go to St Mary's?'

'No. I went to Curraboy National School. And then I went to boarding school in Limerick.'

Villiers, probably. She might be Protestant.

'But we were always in and out of town and we came to

52

Mass in Clonduff,' she says. 'I'm sure our paths crossed there.'

Luke nods.

'My grandfather's name was Luke,' she says then.

'A lovely man, no doubt! Patron saint of doctors.'

She nods, smiles. He can do better than that.

They are both looking at the dog.

'The poor cratur . . .' Luke says.

So much conversation is phatic, social, he thinks. We must be the most accomplished race at saying nothing, and doing it with charm.

'He's very timid . . . worse since Mikey went away. I don't know if he'll ever come right.'

He steals a look at her. Slim, small-chested. Five foot four, at the most. The opposite of Maeve. They wouldn't be a match, physically. He could pick her up.

'Did you say you live in Dublin?'

'Yes, but I come and go.'

'Have you brothers or sisters? Maybe I know them.'

'No brothers. Two sisters, and my mother. My father is dead about five years.'

They are silent then. There is something disquieting about the silence. Suddenly, out of nowhere, he gets an immense feeling of foreboding.

She looks around the room. 'Are you the book-lover in the house?' she asks. When she lifts her eyes to him he swims in them. Green, vivid green. He has to look away.

'I am.'

He waits.

'What do you do?' she asks. 'Are you a farmer?'

'Not really. Well, not at the moment. I lease out the land. I'm a teacher.'

'Ahh,' she says, nodding. 'Primary or secondary?'

'Secondary. English. English and history actually, but mostly English. I teach in Dublin at Belvedere College. I'm on a career break at the moment.'

'Really?' Her eyes widen and she smiles. 'I work in Summerhill and the North Strand area. I'm with the HSE.'

'Ah, you're only up the road from Belevdere then!' They might have passed each other on the street, stood together at a bus stop. 'What do you do in the HSE?' He is trying to avoid looking at her breasts.

'I'm a social worker. Child welfare and protection. I work with kids and teenagers – troubled ones – and their families. And with kids in care. That's my catchment area – the north inner city, your neighbourhood. Very different kids to the ones you teach though, I'd say.'

'A bit, all right. Though we have a few local lads coming to us too.'

They stand looking at the dog. Now the silence becomes a force field around them.

Soon she will leave.

'Poor devil,' he says, about the dog. He sneaks another look at her.

'My mother thought she'd be able to keep him,' she says. 'But our own dog won't tolerate him . . . And this fella is not one to fight his corner. I've been at home on holidays for the last fortnight so he's gotten attached to me. But I can't take him back with me. He'd be alone all day, it wouldn't be fair.'

He leans forward and offers the dog the back of his hand. The dog stiffens with fear. He imagines the little heart beating against the ribcage.

He can keep the dog. He can do what he likes. He can fill the house with dogs, if he likes. No one's business. What people see — the big house overrun with cats, the walls coming down with books, the place going to wrack and ruin.

'I'll keep him,' he says.

'Thank you,' she says. He can hear the gratitude and relief in her voice. 'I'm really grateful.' She looks down at the dog, smiles affectionately. 'You're very lucky, buster! . . . I'll leave you my number and if it doesn't work out I'll come and take him back, I promise. And the girl in SuperValu, Katie, said she'd help — if you need to go away or anything, she said she'd mind him.'

When she stands and draws her body upright his eyes fix on her legs and thighs and he feels a powerful physical sensation, as if he is pulled upwards with her legs and thighs — pulled up by the force of her body, up into her.

She takes her phone from her jeans pocket. He clears his throat. For a moment he cannot recall his phone number, then calls it out haltingly, uncertainly, and she taps her screen. In the hall, his own phone pings.

He stands in the doorway until her yellow car disappears from view. The sun streams into the hall. He listens for sounds inside the house. He steps into the hall and whistles lightly, then calls 'Paddy'. But the dog does not budge. Even when Lily pokes her head around the door he does not stir.

All afternoon Luke leaves him alone. He clatters about the house, opening and closing doors noisily, talking animatedly to Lily. He tries to hear what the dog hears – the distant human voice, the echoes, the footsteps.

Later he enters the drawing room and sits on the sofa, reading. Now and then he tries to coax the dog from his spot. Finally, he lifts him gently – the animal stiffening in his hands – into an old wicker basket and carries him outside to the old servants' kitchen in the yard. He places the basket in a corner where the sun slants in through a high window. He places a bowl of water beside him, and, closing the door behind him, leaves the dog in peace.

IN THE EVENING he walks up the driveway of Ellen's bungalow. Inside, her TV screen flickers in the dim light. He approaches the large picture window and waves, and Ellen rises and beckons him to the front door.

'Is it too late to mow the grass?' he asks, after they greet each other. 'I'll have it done in less than an hour.'

'Ah, there's no need – sure it's hardly a week since you did it last. It's fine, Luke, for another day or two. Come in, come in.'

He watches her walk ahead of him. She had a hip replaced last summer in the Bons Secours Hospital in Cork. He drove her there the day before the operation. In the hospital bed, in her nightdress, she looked nothing like the tall, strong woman of his childhood. Her shoulders, frail and drooping, weighed down, he thought, with eight decades of feeling and worry for the family. When he got up to leave, her eyes suddenly welled up. 'I'll be here in the morning before they take you down to theatre,' he said, bending down to embrace her. She felt like his child then. 'And every day until I bring you home.'

In the living room she zaps the TV off. 'Wouldn't politicians madden you the way they talk, the humming and hawing, the amming and awing? How is it, Luke, in this day and age they can't be more straightforward and articulate? After all the free education, is this what we have, these plebs? The Europeans must be laughing at us beyond in Brussels, with the thick accents and the roundabout way these fools have of saying things.'

'I know. Right gombeen men still, some of them.'

He sits on the sofa opposite her.

'What news have you?" she asks.

She would like to see him settled, married, producing an heir for Ardboe.

He tells her about the dog. 'Katie Cullen in SuperValu sent a girl up with him. His owner – the girl's uncle – is gone into a nursing home. A frightened little fellow he is too.'

The girl is in Dublin by now, back in her own life. All day long since her departure he has felt an absence that he associates with previous partings and separations.

'You and Lucy were always great dog-lovers,' Ellen says.

He nods. He pictures the dog locked in the old kitchen. Moving around on the cold flagstone floor, sniffing at the base of the door. The best thing is to leave him alone until he settles down. 'And Josie, of course,' he says.

'Oh, don't talk,' Ellen replies, rolling her eyes in mock exasperation.

For a few moments, she is, he thinks, pulled back into reverie. As thick as thieves, the two sisters, all their lives. Ellen the protector, Josie the mischief-maker. Slept together in Josie's big bed the first few nights after Ellen's arrival every summer. He'd hear them giggling late at night when he was a boy, and he'd get up and go to them, and climb into bed with them. Ellen giving out about the stink of cats off the bedclothes and the crumbs under them. What're you munching, Josie? Ellen would ask. Nothing. You liary thing, you! You won't have a tooth left in your head, Ellen would admonish, and you're getting fat too. You're going on a diet tomorrow, madam. Now turn around and snuggle up – you too, Luke.

'I met Dilly Madden in town this morning,' he says.

'How is she? Mad as a brush still, I suppose.'

He nods. 'Mad as a brush,' he says, and immediately regrets it.

'God help her, the poor creature.'

'She wasn't always that way, was she?' he asks. 'When she was young?'

'I don't know. I don't remember. But there's a strain in the Maddens. It runs in families.'

'The same might be said of ourselves, Ellen.'

She looks at him, surprised, a little hurt. 'How so? What do you mean?'

'Josie. They could say she was odd, a bit mad.'

'Ah, no, Luke, that's different. Everyone knows why Josie was the way she was. On account of Una's death – the shock of it affected her. Anyway, Josie was just slow. The other thing' — she taps her head — 'is entirely different.' She pauses. 'And Clonduff is full of it, whatever the reason is. I'd bet this whole area has one of the highest rates of mental illness in the whole country.'

Her hands are resting on her lap, her fingers entwined. She rotates her thumbs around each other, first clockwise, then anticlockwise. She has done this for as long as he can remember. He brings his own hands together, holds his thumbs side by side in an upright position. As a child he used to think of his thumbs as human, female, mothers. His fingers were the children, lined up beside them, four kids a-piece. His big toes were mothers too, leaning towards their children. They reminded him of the mosaic image of the Blessed Virgin set into the alcove in the side altar of the church, her head aslant, her face full of patience, kindness, forbearance. Things he has never told anyone. How could he explain that the sight of his own big toes moved him, or that, on certain nights when he pulled aside the covers, he felt a stream of love emanating from them?

'Josie was perfect before the accident,' Ellen explains. 'Sure don't I remember? I was ten at the time. She lost her talk afterwards. We thought she'd never talk again. It was Una's falling into the well that did it.' She looks at Luke. 'My mother was convinced Josie saw it happening. She was only two, but she was out in the yard with Una that morning . . . And then, of course, Dadda's death six months later. It was an awful time for us all . . . an awful time.'

He is on the point of asking her something that has been gnawing at him about the old well.

'Do you know where I was that morning? Above in Lynch's playing with Alice, Jim's sister . . . I was wearing a new green coat that we got for Christmas – Una and I got it between us. That's the way it was, money was scarce, we shared everything . . . I wanted to show off the coat to Alice.'

She jumps up from her armchair. 'I'll make us tea. I made some fruit scones earlier so we'll have some – and you'll take the rest of them home with you.'

Alone, he studies the room. Everything is spotless. Photographs neatly arranged on the mantelpiece and on the wall: Ellen and her mother on a trip to Knock years ago; his father and mother on their wedding day; several photos of Josie and Lucy and himself; various members of the Clark family, the wealthy American family who were Ellen's employers for almost forty years. During the day she keeps the TV tuned to CNN, the volume set low or on mute, the loop of American news and images streaming into her room her way of staying in touch with America. She retired and moved home when she was sixty-four and had this bungalow – a retirement gift from the Clarks – built on the family land.

During her trips home every summer Ellen brought her American ways with her. She taught him and Lucy to make cookies and peach pie and knickerbocker glories. She brought home a red soda fountain, a cheese board, a coffee percolator. She taught them how to set the table properly. Always wanting to improve them, help them better themselves. She bought him his first watch. She brought books, small musical instruments – ukuleles, flutes. Beautiful American clothes – dungarees, sneakers, baseball caps, the expensive cast-offs of the Clark children. Occasionally, still, Luke wears the perfectly preserved cord jackets and sweaters once worn by Hubie Clark in the 1960s and '70s.

She carries in a tray with tea and scones. She picks up a teaspoon and hands it to him.

'Take a good look at that,' she says.

He turns the spoon over. 'Ah, Aer Lingus! I remember! You used to steal the spoons on the plane, you thief, you! There's still one left above in the house.'

'They're the only things I ever stole in my whole life. A spoon a year – when Aer Lingus still served proper cutlery. And I don't regret it one bit. After all I spent on Aer Lingus airfares over the years!'

She pours the tea.

'Do you want to go to Waterford or anywhere this week?' he asks. 'What about Cork? Do you feel like a browse around the shops?'

She has mild blood pressure and some arthritis in the other hip but she is, otherwise, healthy. She takes a daily walk by the river or up the road to the graveyard. She rarely goes into the town. He brings her groceries from SuperValu several times a week. Her service to others has long ended. Once, she was engaged to be married. Though full of goodness and generosity her whole life he has the impression that, privately, she is a little bitter, and thinks life went against her.

'Ah, I'm all right for now. Sure what do I need? Aren't

the wardrobes below there full of clothes?' she says. 'I have an appointment with the eye clinic in Waterford next Thursday, eleven o'clock I think. We'll go for a nice lunch afterwards, if you're not in a hurry.' Then, pausing before she lifts her cup, she says, 'You poor devil, you'll have spent your best years driving old women to hospital appointments.'

What of it, he wants to say. He couldn't not do it. It used to perplex Maeve, his duty-boundness, as she called it. It's not duty, he'd correct her, duty demands effort. Besides, he wanted to say, I get more than I give.

And he'd have driven Josie to Timbuktu if he thought it would save her. The hope he had had that late spring and early summer, driving her up to the hospital in Cork. Four days a week for five weeks. Desperately willing the treatment to work. Praying even. The drive over the Vee where he pulled over and stopped one morning and pointed out the three counties below them. That's Cork over there, he said. A stony silence from Josie then, an atmosphere that usually indicated hurt or confusion. No, it's not, she said, Cork is pink. It took him a few seconds to realise she was remembering the counties as he had taught her years ago using a political map of Ireland. Driving through the sleepy towns and villages along the way, a gentle silence settling on them. Will we stop for an ice cream, he'd ask. Then they'd sit in the car with the windows down, licking their ice cream cones, gazing at a tractor going by or a small group of children on the footpath. Without saying a word, one of them would start to suck the ice cream noisily from the tip of the wafer, and the other would join in. You're an awful woman, Josie O'Brien, he'd say. He'd walk her along the hospital corridor to the cancer ward, watch her face suddenly darken with rage if her favourite infusion chair was occupied by another patient. When the nurse inserted the IV line Josie would turn to him. 'You can go now, Luke.' On the occasions when he was mistaken for her son, neither of them corrected the error. He remembers how every Friday evening for years she got all dolled up before he arrived home from Dublin. Following his mother around, pestering her with questions – what time is it, why isn't he here – until his mother would lash out. You're a scourge! A silly old woman! Where do you think he is – above in Dublin enjoying himself with Maeve, that's where! Each leave-taking wounded her. She cried at the door every Sunday evening when he left to return to the city.

'Old women, my eye!' he says. 'After all you did for us, Ellen, over the years.'

'Do you know my one regret?' she says.

He shakes his head. Not having children of her own, he guesses, but it's unlikely she'll say that.

'Not learning to drive. A big mistake. But in America I always had Ernest the chauffeur to take me everywhere. And then when I came home every summer, your mother drove me around.'

On the mornings of Ellen's arrival his mother rose early and drove up to Shannon to meet her. All morning Josie waited at an upstairs window for the first sighting of the car coming up the avenue, then came running down the stairs shouting, *They're here, they're here.* A great welcome at the front door then. Huge suitcases thrown open in the hall. Toys, clothes, candy. Smell of mothballs. Chatter and laughter drifting up from the kitchen. Ellen home, the family made whole again. He remembers the purity of that joy. He wishes he could find a way back to that place and those times and resurrect the family's past, its dimmed glory.

'I tried to get your mother and father to come out and visit me in America before ye kids were born. Your mother would have come in a shot.' She snaps her fingers. 'But your father was afraid of flying.'

'And driving. And heights,' Luke says. 'He wouldn't even climb a ladder to paint the house. Mammy had no fear, she ran up and down the ladder like a mountain goat.'

'He climbed Croagh Patrick once.'

'He did not! I didn't know that.'

'A whole gang of us went . . . Lord God, where have the years gone? In the early years when I was home we'd often go on some pilgrimage. We were all very pious then, everyone went to Mass and Confessions. They were social outings too, you know, a way of meeting people. All innocent fun. Later on, after your father got married, your mother drove us on our little outings. You won't remember them, most of them were before you or Lucy were born.'

'I do remember. We went to Ballinspittle to see the moving statue one summer, all of us packed into the car. I was about six. Do you remember that?'

She stares at him, as if trying to call it up. She nods slowly.

'Where was Josie then?' he asks. 'Did we leave her at home

65

on her own, Ellen?' Josie was absent from other family outings too – trips to Cork on Saturdays throughout his childhood, his mother at the wheel, his father beside her, Luke and Lucy in the back. They'd stop off at the Silver Springs Hotel on the way into the city for their lunch. One Saturday his father bought his mother a purple coat in Cash's. It was on those trips during his teenage years that he started to buy books. All that time, Josie was home alone. Standing at the landing window for hours, waiting for the lights of the car to come up the avenue. No question of not coming back to look after her when she got sick. Maeve had protested. Why can't your mother drive her to the hospital? Why do *you* have to take two months off work to do it? The good was gone by then, he and Maeve had reached their natural end and this – Maeve's jealousy – was the final straw. Josie had put a pack of sanitary towels into the shopping trolley in SuperValu one Tuesday during the weekly shop. What d'you want them for, his mother asked. Mind your own business. On the way home she said her month-lies were back. She might have been bleeding for months, or longer, before she said anything. Afraid of his mother's ridicule.

Ellen has not answered him. She, too, is in a drift of thoughts.

'Have you heard from the Clarks lately?' he asks.

'Nothing since Christmas.' Hubie and Flo, once her young charges, write every Christmas with all the news. There was a time when the names of the Clark children were as familiar to him as his own sister's. 'They're busy with their own lives, I suppose. Their kids are grown up now, of course. Hubie has a little grandson . . . How the years fly.'

'They do,' he says.

She nods, then grows pensive.

'Family is everything,' she says quietly. 'Blood is everything.' Her voice is remote. Thinking of his mother, Sarah, maybe, who was not blood to her. Two strong women, once as close as sisters, growing gradually hostile towards each other over the years. From long summers spent sharing the kitchen, the initial joy of annual reunions turning to antagonism. Ellen critical of Sarah's housekeeping and mothering skills. It's none of your business how I rear my children. Later, after his father's death and no one now to rein in his mother, Ellen didn't hold back. You're a holy show, a disgrace to this family. Words spoken that were never taken back.

'There's something I often meant to ask you,' he says and waits for her to look at him. 'Isn't it strange that Dadda never covered in the well after Lucy and I were born? I often wondered why — considering how protective of us he was.'

She frowns. 'Is it not covered? It's years since I was down in the yard but I thought there was a cover on it.'

He shakes his head. 'There's a wooden pallet sitting on the top, that's all. I never remember anything else covering it. When the pallet rotted he'd replace it with another pallet, and now I do the same. If Lucy ever comes home with her kids I'll have it properly capped with concrete.'

'Well, that is strange because, Lord, ye were the apples of his eye. I wonder if there was some reason. Maybe he thought it was bad luck. On account of Una.'

She seems distracted for a few moments. 'I think there must be underground channels running from the well down to the river. Years ago when I was young the river broke its banks and flooded the town, and Ardboe was flooded too but the water didn't come over the land, it came up from underground, from somewhere around the house. Maybe from the well. I don't know how it happened. There must be some underground connection.'

He had never heard about this. The river occasionally breaks its banks but Ardboe is far enough away to avoid being flooded. He remembers the ship's windows in the east wing. The whole place has a watery dimension.

They sit in peaceful silence. Her presence moves him. She is like a mother to him.

'Are you sleeping well these times, Luke?' she asks. Last winter she had noticed him looking tired and he had admitted that he was sleeping poorly. The next day, she handed him a packet of melatonin tablets. 'They're a natural remedy, they're not addictive.' She had walked into town to her GP, pretended she had insomnia and got a prescription for them.

'I am. I stay up too late reading, but I sleep fine. What about you?'

'I don't usually have trouble sleeping, but lately – I don't know why – I couldn't sleep at all last night. I suppose it's my age. And I'm dwelling too much on the past, too, going over and over things in my head. Do you do that? . . . No, you're too young to have those kinds of thoughts. Last night, for some reason, I thought of a poem I found in Hubie Clark's bedroom years ago – when he was a teenager. It's one thing I've never forgotten – it often pops into my mind . . . I picked it up off the floor, it was typed so I thought Hubie himself had written it for school. The man in the poem was called Henry – I always remember refined names like that. Anyway Henry was plagued by a recurring dream. In the dream he killed someone and the dream felt so real that when he woke up he was sure it was true and he really had killed someone. But then he counted everyone, and no one was missing. No one was ever missing.'

For a few moments there is, on her face, a look of bafflement. What is it she is thinking?

'What else kept you awake last night?' he asks. 'What else were you thinking about?'

'About how different everything is, how there's only you and me left now. I doubt Lucy will ever come back to live here. I never expected to be on my own all my life. I was thinking last night about Josie too, and Una and Dadda's sudden death. All of that.' She looks at him. 'I have this thought sometimes, this notion . . . that maybe I took a wrong turn somewhere along the way – or maybe the family took a wrong turn in the past. When I think of the fine family that we were, and all those who went before us and the big estate my mother came from. My grandmother, my mother's mother, went to a private school in France when she was a young woman! Imagine that! She could speak fluent French and play the piano. Did you know that, Luke? That's the kind of lineage we have! My mother could play the piano. Of course it was a big come-down for her marrying my father. Maybe that was the wrong turning.'

And Dadda's marriage, another come-down, she probably thinks, though she doesn't say it.

'Losing Una was terrible,' he says, 'and then your father, but lots of families have tragedies, Ellen, and some a lot worse than that. It doesn't have to be caused by a wrong turn.'

'I suppose.'

'And you shouldn't be hard on yourself either. Jesus, Ellen – you've spent your whole life helping others. Sending money home to your mother in the early years, coming home every summer to help out with the work. And helping Dadda too. Remember when he got that big arrears bill from Revenue and you bailed him out? Remember? And he sowed a field of potatoes in your honour to thank you!'

Managing money, never one of Dadda's gifts. Nor his, either.

'I know. I was always trying to do the best for everyone. In America years ago I'd be awake at night worrying about things – Mamma's blood pressure or Josie's epilepsy or how they were going to make ends meet if the price of milk or beet fell. I was always a worrier. You can grow demented thinking about things, I know that. And last night for some reason I started going back in time, trying to put my finger on the exact moment that things started to go wrong. You know the way they say a person often comes to a fork in the road and they have to decide? Well, maybe I should never have gone to America. Or – and don't laugh at this, Luke – when I was a girl I thought I had a religious vocation and I pushed it away. I might have been a reverend mother!' She lets out a fine hearty laugh and he laughs with her.

'Sister Ellen,' he says, smiling.

Suddenly he remembers Joyce's governess . . . Dante whatshername in Bray. As a little boy he sat at her feet as she recited poetry. She wanted to be a nun too, but she got taken in by a bank clerk from the Bank of Ireland and married him, and then he made off with her fortune. Abandoned bride. Conway her name was. Conman Conway. Women can be awful gullible.

'Anyway, who knows,' Ellen says. 'But last night I kept going back . . . back to Dadda's death and Josie's muteness, back to New Year's Day in 1941. That was the day that changed everything for this family. We never really talked about it. But I remember it well.'

All the memories she has that he knows nothing about. How we can be so close and yet.

'Tell me,' he says. 'Tell me what happened.'

'It was one of those cold winter mornings, frost on the windowpanes. I remember coming down into the warm steamy kitchen, my father at the table, Josie laughing – her little baby laugh. The kettle boiling and the tea poured and none of us realising how close we were to the calamity . . . But the clock was ticking. I re-live it so often in my mind

– Dadda rising from his chair, reaching for his hat . . . heading towards the disaster that was less than half an hour away. And all I wanted was to get up to Lynch's as fast as I could to show off the new coat to Alice.'

She looks at Luke, shakes her head.

'When I got home they were bringing her up out of the well. They had tied a rope around Dadda's waist and he went down and brought her up and handed her to the men . . . limp. And do you know the worst of it, Luke? Do you know what my first thought was? I thought wasn't it a good job I wore the new coat up to Lynch's because look at the blood and muck on that one. Now I'd have the new one all to myself . . .' She pauses. 'I often think – suppose it was Una, and not me, who had skived off up to Lynch's that morning in the new coat? Suppose it was me and not Una who went out to do the chores – gathering the eggs, bringing in the turf? That's what I was imagining last night . . . Me crossing the yard that morning after collecting the eggs, me heading toward the house but stopping at the well, leaning over the wall, looking in. And Josie with me, lagging behind, playing with the cat maybe . . . And supposing the well was destined to claim a child that day – any child. No matter what, it was preordained. I began to rewind every-thing that happened that morning, like when they run a film backwards and I brought Una up out of the well, and mended her bones and walked her back across the yard to the henhouse and the turf-shed, and back up into the house, and there I was – the other me, sitting at the table. And I swapped places and steered that me towards the back door and out across the yard to the life about to be snuffed out.'

He can see it all. The yard, the well, the little girl. He wants to say no, nothing was preordained, but the words won't come.

'Lying in bed last night,' she says, 'it came to me: *Una was the lucky one.* To have died young, without blemish. Dispatched straight to Heaven with the pure heart of a child, to have suffered only broken bones, a broken body. To be spared the struggles of growing up and growing old, spared all that heartache. Isn't it true, Luke? And do you know what else I thought? I thought that in another moral universe, I might hold Una accountable for all we have suffered. Accountable for Dadda's death too and all that came after, and for the breach in Josie — for the way her brain was affected and her life changed for ever . . .'

He is walking home in the late evening. Sing, Josie would say, as they crested the Vee on the journey home. The nausea would still be hours or even days away. They were back in their own county, the sun low, the valley opening out before them. Below, in the distance, the road and the winding river will lead them home. He'd think of the chemicals coursing through her veins, the poison infusing her cells. Then he'd clear his throat and throw her a smile, and she, *she*, would sit up straight, her head held high, proud to be the one giving the orders, and being obeyed. Drumming his hand on the steering wheel he'd begin to hum the intro. After a few bars he'd break into song and she would follow suit. *I have climbed highest mountains, I have run through the fields.*

He can feel the river's presence on his right. It never leaves him; it is there, always, on the edge of his consciousness. Even in sleep, it flows through his dreams, watching, waiting, coaxing his attention. He stands and gazes at the water. The tide is coming up, gently, barely perceptible. Twelve miles from the sea and still tidal, every drop still governable by the moon. And inside every drop, millions of atoms in perpetual motion. No, trillions. He calculated the figure one night when he was a teenager. He had to compute the molar mass of water first and then use Avogrado's Number to get the number of molecules. And then he must have followed some other formula to arrive at the number of atoms. Deep into the machinery of number, he used to feel enlarged, exhilarated, feel himself and the world cohere. He's forgotten it all now . . . Sextillions it was, not trillions. Sextillions of atoms inside every drop of water and inside each atom, a riot of commotion and collision. And all the atoms in all the drops in all the oceans and seas and rivers and lakes, in streams and ponds and puddles, in tanks and pipes and taps, in kettles, bottles, glasses, beakers, tin cans . . . the constant motion, the perpetual striving of water. Towards what?

He walks on. Any minute now, the tide will turn at the Inch and begin its outward journey. He would like to arrest time at that moment of turning, witness the instant the change occurs and the current swirls and turns and begins to slide back towards the sea. He tilts his head to listen

74

closely. The turn of the tide must be discernible to certain creatures, the low liquid decibels audible to the ears of dippers, maybe, and otters and swans. A sound discernible to trees and plants too. The kind of thing Josie might have heard.

He turns and looks downriver. In the dusk the river melds with the bank and the woodlands. He can make out the old chicken factory in the distance. A time will come when it will be a roofless edifice, with jackdaws flying in under steel girders, the ground littered with puny bones and old manure, a feather floating in the air.

He walks on. He thinks about the girl. Ruth. He lets the name form in his mind. What is it he feels? A gathering of desire, a great urge to see her. To see her naked, to be inside her. He has been celibate for two years, since he and Deirdre Kelly from the council estate outside the town comforted each other for a few weeks, each in the aftermath of their mothers' deaths.

He really should move back to Dublin. Dublin. In the magical chaos after Josie's death he had returned to his job in Belvedere. Then slowly, over a year, he began to suffer a progressive erosion of the spirit, a steady depletion of reserves. Without Maeve he lost the run of himself and the city became a place of freedom and temptation and excess. He drank copiously, spent with abandon, sated old appetites. New desires too. On a staff night out, in the dark corner of a nightclub, the young, newly appointed maths teacher, Oisín Kelly, with his fair to reddish hair and delicate cheekbones and tired misty eyes, put a hand on Luke's arm and looked steadily into his eyes. In the late-night heady mix of dim lights and music and alcohol, he thought Oisín beautiful. Oisín smiled and leaned in and kissed him on the mouth and he kissed him back, and then panicked.

'I'm not gay,' he said.

Oisín smiled and shrugged. 'So?'

'That's the truth! I swear! If I was gay I'd have been out at fifteen.'

Jesus Christ, he thought, what am I? Half gay?

It was true: if he were gay he would have been out at fifteen. He would not have cared. He is his father's son — tell the truth at all costs, regardless of convention.

He looked at Oisín, at one of his eyes, then the other, at the smiling mouth, and he kissed him again. Desire rising in the tongue and the mouth, lust in the groin; physical love bred out of spirit and intellect and beauty. Walking in the small hours through empty streets to Oisín's place, the bawdy talk, the wicked laughter. His hand on a man's cock. Jesus, to hold a cock that wasn't his own. The tender touch of Oisín's hand, his lips, the tawny hair on his arms in the dawn light. And then the walk home alone in daylight and the shock, the sickly realisation, of what he had done.

But the next day he returned to Oisín and to days and nights of pure joy and laughter and ecstasy, moments of love and of feeling newly born. Followed by hours of self-loathing, fear, doubt, panic at being spotted entering a gay bar. He began to admire men's bodies, their bare arms, square shoulders, round tight arses. He began to dress differently, take care of his skin. Mother of God. When he was with Oisín it wasn't tawdry, but natural. Just sitting together meant something. It was more than sex. He didn't know how to describe it.

Why do we have to be one thing or the other? he thinks. Why do we have to be anything? Does it matter who we kiss, who fills us with longing? Does it matter who puts what where? The thing he had not foreseen, not expected, was the purity of feeling, the integrity of feeling he had for men. Way beyond the physical, beyond mere possession. To do with the ease and affinity between men, the protectiveness, the feeling that he could say anything and do anything and nothing had to be explained.

One of the first signs of the end of the world, he read once: when men marry men. For a few years it was where the heat was: inside a man, at the source, the nub, the core. The need to touch and be touched there. He has always loved human touch, human skin, human smells. In the nine months he was with Oisín he oscillated between moments of searing shame and fear and uncertainty, and the thrill of new adventure, the feeling of opening doors, flinging up windows. Extreme feeling this, living from the heart of the sensorium. He read widely about sexuality, mulled over his own, acted out his craven fantasies. Alone, he contemplated the feminine in himself and, stirred by desire at the thought of being part woman, he massaged his nipples, ran a finger along his scrotal scar, the vestigial seam of a foetal vagina before its folds fused and his pre-natal self became male. *Baculum, baubellum.* He imagined his own labia, a tight cervix, his unborn womb an ocean of fecundity. He detected a sensitive and feminine element in himself, and suspected that, at certain times of the month, he still possessed traces of a rudimentary menstrual cycle that, prone to the pull of celestial bodies, affected his entire organism.

The pendulum swung back. He could not bear the thought of being without woman – the carnal pleasures, the emotional intimacies, the feeling of completeness. But the door had opened and he could not unknow all he now knew, or unfeel all he felt. And he was the better for it and would not be without this knowledge and experience. He has a theory that the current states of male and female are transitional, intermediary, that mankind is still evolving, and that human evolution will eventually culminate in a single form that contains and integrates both male and female elements in a sophisticated hermaphroditic self. He is convinced the evolutionary pressure is increasing and change is imminent, and he finds the idea of such change philosophically and aesthetically pleasing.

Up ahead in the twilight, the old iron railway bridge soars high above the road. Soon the stars will rise and brighten. On the far bank of the river the willows lean low over the water, and behind them the old oak and beech trees exude a powerful feeling of sadness. He peers into the darkness beyond, imagining the eyes of creatures looking out from fringed ferns and mosses. His thoughts are pulled under to where the mundane world gives way to another dimension. Rocks and roots and drowned men's bones on the riverbed, boughs, branches, the hulls of old boats resting at angles of repose. Reeds and rushes and pondweed waving in the cold, murky darkness as little currents and eddies mysteriously arrive and depart, before an eerie peace is restored again. He imagines it all, imagines a time before the river ran through this naked earth, before flowers and glaciers, before the age of reptiles. He feels himself a protean creature and there is something he is meant to understand in that watery world, something fugitive and fleeting and very old.

RUTH CALLS HIM the following evening. 'So, how's your new charge doing?'

'He's still a bit wary,' Luke tells her. 'But he'll come round. And he's eating now, which is a good sign.'

For a few minutes they talk about the dog. They slip into natural conversation with ease, as if they've known each other for a long time. They talk about Dublin – the pubs and restaurants they both know – and Clonduff, and each other. Her family farm, three miles from Ardboe, is run by her sister and her sister's husband. She went to university in Cork. She lives in Rathfarnham and spends an hour and twenty minutes in traffic every morning.

She calls again the next evening. They talk for an hour. She tells him she'll be visiting her mother at the weekend and could drop by to see Paddy, if it suited him. When he hangs up, he crosses the kitchen with a spring in his step, and circles Saturday on the calendar.

*　　*　　*

'See that corner?' he says, pointing to the field below.

It is Saturday and they are walking along a headland, the dog at their heels. 'There's a sinkhole down there, to the right.' He stops, leans towards her and points at a spot in the distance. 'See the dip in the land? One morning when I was about eight we came out here to find the ground had caved in overnight. No forewarning – it had been a perfectly ordinary green field the day before.'

'I never heard of a sinkhole,' she says, frowning. 'We have a turlough on our land. My sisters and I were always afraid to go too near it when we were kids. Lambs and sheep got sucked down into it, my father said. Maybe he just said that to keep us away from it.'

She leans down and touches the dog's head and he runs off ahead of them and sniffs in the undergrowth. He's a different dog since she arrived.

She frowns often, in concentration, just before she speaks. Stop that frowning, he wants to say, you'll get wrinkles. Already, starting to look out for her. He shouldn't do that.

She's looking south, to the hills beyond Collon whose slopes are dotted with windmills. You're lovely, he wants to say.

'The wind farms are popping up everywhere, aren't they,' she says. 'They're over our way too.'

'They're ruining this valley. I can't abide them, or the pylons. I objected to them all in the planning stages, but to no avail.' There was a time, a few years ago, when he was consumed by wind farms, constantly on the lookout for new ones on hillsides as he was driving. He went around the town drumming up support for a protest or petition until finally the council called a public meeting, at which he spoke. He briefly flirted with the idea of running for election, going into politics. His father's imprint on him, the impulse to serve.

'I hate pylons too,' she says. 'I don't think the windmills are as bad.'

'But they're ugly-looking brutes.'

'That's maybe because you have a very refined sense of the aesthetic, Mr O'Brien!'

He smiles, and then jostles her playfully. They talk again about the city. At the mention of place-names his mind roams the streets. She walks the pier in Dún Laoghaire on Saturdays. She mentions friends, but never a boyfriend.

They are walking side by side, her legs extending along-side his, almost touching. He takes shorter strides to keep in step. He thinks of her bare legs inside her jeans. She walks a step or two ahead of him. Nice round bottom, no visible panty line. Hate that word, panties. Too American. Something smutty and pervy sounding about it. Prefer the hearty Irish knickers. Imagine her slipping them off . . . *her soft vagina*. The words from a book that gave him his first erection at twelve or thirteen. *A Thousand and One Nights*, maybe. A harem, a young master returns to his private quarters after a long day, passing though internal courtyards and a corridor of cells where the soft vaginas of his concu-bines await him.

They trudge up the incline in the middle of the field. When he turns around he sees Ellen at the clothesline behind her house. The wind blows up from the river. Scudding clouds pass overhead. He steals a look at Ruth. Hebrew name. The name evokes thoughtfulness. Cannot imagine a Ruth who isn't kind.

The air brightens. The sun breaks through and running shadows chase the fields. In the distance, the town, the church spire, Blake's hill crowned with oaks. They stand and look back the way they came, at the house and the avenue.

'We weren't always here,' he says, looking at her. 'My family, I mean. We're not landed gentry.'

'No?' she says, teasingly.

He smiles. 'Can't you tell?'

They are walking along the boundary wall towards the quarry.

'The first Luke O'Brien came over the Knockmealdowns from Tipperary, on foot,' he says, 'sometime in the late 1890s, and dropped down into the Sullane valley. He was only sixteen. Apparently he made his way out to the Ardglass peninsula and appeared unheralded at the front door of Valentine and Alicia Bagenal. Or so the story goes! The Bagenals were landlords; they had a huge estate – over ten thousand acres at one stage.' He stops and looks at her, fearful of overstating his pedigree.

'I've often passed by here,' she says. 'My father is buried in the graveyard up the road there and I just assumed – because of the long avenue and the big house – that this was an Anglo-Irish, Protestant place, like all the others.'

'My grandmother was Protestant, she converted to marry

84

my grandfather,' he says. A thought strikes him, a coincidence: If, like in Judaism, Christianity had followed matrilineal descent, he would be severed from his source religion at the paternal grandmother stage. Just like Leopold Bloom.

'Family lore has it that Luke – after reaching Ardglass – found a grey stallion straying on the road. He used a piece of old rope to fashion a bridle and then walked the stallion up to the hall door of Bagenal's manor house and somehow gained a foothold there – first in the household, and eventually, years later, in the heart of the only child in the family, Elizabeth Alicia Bagenal, my grandmother. He must have acquitted himself fairly well, because they got a fine house built and four hundred acres of land at Coole Quay, two miles downriver from here, as a wedding gift. They moved up here to this place in 1928.'

'So ye're castle Catholics, then.'

'Mongrels, more like. And this place is smaller than the Coole place, so it must've been a bit of a come-down.' He never knew if the land at Coole was sold or lost or swapped, or why his grandfather moved the family to Ardboe. These are questions he wishes he had asked his father, ones which he must remember to ask Ellen sometime.

'Still, not bad for the descendants of a young lad who came over the mountains,' she says.

'Not bad at all!' He gives her a broad smile. 'The lad brought no one with him from Tipperary and never went back, and nothing of his past life was ever known. So we have to attribute all our congenital faults and failings to the Bagenal side of the family.'

He has read the records at Waterford Museum. The Bagenals were tough landlords, merciless when it came to evictions. The knowledge that a propensity for cruelty runs through his bloodline sometimes disturbs him.

'I often imagine – it's a hunch I have – that, in the long tradition of risk-takers and chancers and those seeking their fortunes, my grandfather might have hopped into a field that day and *led* the stallion out and up to the big house. Which would mean', he says, smiling wryly, 'that the foundation of the union – the foundation of this whole family – is based on a fabrication, a deceit!'

He offers her a hand when they climb over rocks. The way she hops down, like a young girl, delights him. His mind is racing with thoughts of how to delay her departure.

'Are you in a hurry?' he asks. 'Would you like to stay for dinner? I can rustle up a mean steak and mashed potato, if you'd care for it?'

She looks down. His heart sinks.

When she lifts her face, she is smiling. 'I don't eat meat but mashed potato will do the job,' she says, a little apologetically.

'Ah, a vegetarian? What about fish?'

She shakes her head. 'No fish either. But I swear, when it comes to mashed potatoes I could eat you out of house and home!'

'Well, in that case – and,' he says with a flourish, 'if you'll deign to dine with a man who might be descended from an imposter – let us proceed!'

He puts on some jazz. They work together, she frying garlic, onion and tomatoes, he cooking pasta.

'How long are you a vegetarian?'

'Since I was fifteen. My father found a pup abandoned in a ditch one day and brought her home. Tammy. She was the first dog we ever kept indoors. Anyway, almost immediately I went off meat.'

'Because?'

'It didn't make sense to eat meat any more. I thought: how can I eat a little lamb and not eat Tammy?'

'That's very admirable.' He is nodding, frowning a little. He wants to say something more, that he too identifies with her feeling for animals. Even as the thought arrives he can hear how hollow it would sound.

'There's nothing admirable about it – giving up meat was no sacrifice for me. Honestly, it's a lot easier for me *not* to eat meat. All my family eat meat. I probably come from one of the biggest meat-eating families in the county! And I ate enough meat in my first fifteen years to last me a lifetime. Look' – she offers her arm – 'if you press here I'll moo! And I was reared and educated on the backs of slaughtered animals.'

'Jesus, when you put it like that.'

'It was all very painful for a long time. I read everything – the philosophy, the accounts of animal experiments and vivisections. I was consumed. I saw animal suffering everywhere. On the city streets, on the journey home at weekends – hungry horses in mucky fields, livestock trucks packed with cattle or sheep, a circus parked on the edge of some town, the animals locked up in dark containers twenty-three hours a day.' She stops suddenly. 'Anyway, enough of that!'

He is opening a bottle of red wine.

'Can I tempt you? You could leave your car here and call Dillon's. Or, if you like, you're welcome to stay over – there are five spare bedrooms up there to choose from.'

'Oh, go on then. I'll have a small glass. I can still drive with one.'

She eats slowly, small forkfuls of pasta. He does the same. Tasty dish, he thinks. Will leave a nice aftertaste of garlic.

She leaves her fork down before talking. His mother used to talk with her mouth full. Her teeth are small, white, even. He watches her chew. He should give up meat. He's vegetarian in mind and spirit anyway. How to reconcile eating meat with mercy for animals? Impossible. Ashamed whenever he allows himself to think about it. Weak in will, in body. Too much appetite. Need to curb the base appetites, refine the soul.

She is telling him about her sisters, both older. Rosaleen the eldest, married to Gabriel, inherited the family farm. The middle sister, Kathy, is a teacher in Cork. Three sisters. He wonders if they look alike . . . The dark-haired Mulvey sisters. Could make a ballad out of it, like 'The Galway Girl'. 'The Lass of Aughrim'. *If you'll be the . . . as I'm taking you mean to be . . .*

He makes them coffee. He tells her about Lucy in Australia, his mother's death.

'So why did you take a career break?' she asks. 'Was it for a specific purpose?'

The sudden pressure to justify this idle life, to explain who and what he is now. A man without a job or a mule or a mission.

'I took a few months' unpaid leave to look after Josie when she was ill. Then, after she died, I went back to work for a year before taking the career break. I had – have – this idea for a book on James Joyce that I'm working on. Well, at times. But I spent the first year or two doing up the house – the interior. I've to tackle the exterior yet, as you can tell. I put in a new bathroom, got new light fittings, new carpets . . . Spent all my savings at auctions!'

'The house is lovely, you did a great job.'

'Then, one year led to the next and before I knew it, here I am into the final year. So I'll probably be back in school next year. It's either that or resign my permanent job. I have to let the principal know by January.'

They move to the drawing room, carrying their mugs. He switches on the lamps.

'Ah-ha!' she says, inspecting one of the shelves. 'I can see the fondness for Joyce.'

'The love of my life . . . to date.' He smiles mischievously. Time to take things up a notch. 'Joyce and my aunt Josie, my two great loves,' he adds.

She tilts her head to read the titles along one shelf, then removes a book.

'*Pox: Genius, Madness and the Mysteries of Syphilis.*' She gives him an amused look. 'Interesting reading material!'

Stick with me, baby, he wants to say, I won't bore you.

She flicks through the pages. 'Abraham Lincoln had syphilis? Jesus. And Hitler. Holy moly . . . And Joyce!' She looks at him, incredulous. 'No!'

'Afraid so.'

'Jesus,' she whispers, flicking back to the contents page, then forward to the index. 'All the geniuses . . . I knew about Nietzsche and Beethoven and poor Karen Blixen getting it off the husband. But all these . . .'

A little shiver runs through him. He became obsessed with syphilis after he discovered Joyce had it and spent hours online reading about it. *Treponema pallidum.* A type of bacterium called a spirochete. A parasite that slips through the warm moist skin of the genitals. All the suffering it caused for centuries, all the havoc it wreaked in people's lives. In existence for eons, before crossing the species divide. Found in a twenty-million-year-old fossil – trapped in the airtight guts of a termite. Wreaking the same havoc in the lives of termites or gnats or mice. Everything is relative.

'But Joyce?' She's frowning again. 'Is it generally known he had it?'

'It was sometimes speculated about. More has been written about it lately, but it's painful stuff. And Stephen, his grandson, is still alive and lives in Paris. He has a reputation for being difficult – and fiercely protective of Joyce. And can you blame him? I would too, if I were him.'

Must be nearly eighty now, Stephen Joyce. The last link. Called his granddad Nonno. Holding Nonno's hand as a little boy going along the street. Touch of the hand still on him. Nonno wrote him a story about a cat and Alfie Byrne, the Lord Mayor of Dublin. Sent him a little cat filled with sweets. *My dear Stevie.*

'How did he catch it?' she asks. 'From prostitutes?'

'Probably.'

Suddenly, he feels disloyal, like he's talking about his own father. Slightly sick too. Doesn't like to think of all the suffering. And no cure until penicillin. Sir Alexander Fleming. A farmer's son from Ayrshire. He married a nurse from Mayo. All the good one person can bring into the world. Works the other way too. Alas, his cure came too late for Joyce.

'Come on, have your coffee,' he says.

She puts the book back, sits on the sofa, he on the armchair. For a while they are silent. He is nervous, out of practice. Do what you always did, he thinks.

'So, Miss Veggie . . . how old are you?'

'I'm thirty-six. And you?'

'Thirty-four.'

'Single?'

She nods. '*Et toi, Monsieur?*'

He nods. 'Also single.'

They smile at each other.

'For long? If I may be so bold to ask?' he says.

'Ooh, almost four years. I'm divorced, actually. I was married for eight years.'

He did not see that coming. A husband. Ex-husband.

'Kids?'

She shakes her head. 'No. Now, your turn.'

'Never married. A five-year relationship ended in my late

91

twenties, and since then . . . a few short-term ones. Nothing serious.' He pauses. Never a right time to divulge the other. Best to get it over with at the start. Then they know. 'The last girl I was out with was about two years ago.'

Her eyes are fixed on him.

His heart is thumping. 'Something else . . . full disclosure.'

Nothing to lose at this stage. Remember Dadda: the truth at all costs. Not that he always reveals this. Only when he really likes . . . Madness, this. She'll hightail it out the door, like the girl from Cork last year.

'I'm attracted to both men and women,' he says. He pauses, scans her face for a reaction. 'Though I've dated mostly women and my longest relationship was with a woman.' Always the need to mitigate.

Her face is completely composed, neutral, betraying nothing. Not as much as a blink. If she's shocked she's hiding it well.

'So you're bisexual. You identify as bisexual.' Again, a neutral tone. Not a question, a statement.

He shrugs. He has been here before. I identify as me, he wants to say. 'I like to think of myself as just . . . sexual, not bisexual or straight or gay or any other label.' Trying not to sound defensive.

She looks down. Impossible to know what she's thinking. All the knowledge we can access, but the mind of another is still impenetrable.

'I don't like to categorise gender or pigeonhole human attraction,' he says. 'The old paradigm of gender is irrelevant, yes. Sexuality is not immutable and, well, we're all human and – you know that saying – nothing human is unnatural?'

He has spoken softly, with a conciliatory tone, but the atmosphere is changed, the mood graver. What did he expect? Hardly comedy, this.

'So when – have you always . . .?'

Her tone is distant, impersonal, almost professional. She'll feign an interest now for a while, then skedaddle.

'No. Not until I was twenty-seven. I always liked men, admired their bodies, loved their minds, their company . . . just like I did women. But I never . . . kissed a guy or anything. Then I was out one night with a friend and . . . it just happened. The old cliché – it started with a kiss.'

Nothing to lose now. He can see it in her eyes – she's gone. Always a problem for women. Gay sex. See it as gross. Most women wouldn't touch him with a forty-foot pole. Thinking of him shoving his . . . Younger women are more open. Gay men don't mind as much – they don't believe in bi anyway. Want to give every man the gay card.

'Out of the blue, just like that?' she asks. A new note in her voice, faintly irritated, a hint of accusation, or doubt even.

'If you mean was I, or am I, a latent homosexual, then no. If I was gay, I'd have been out at fifteen. I had tolerant parents – understanding parents. They never believed in repressing the truth. And what other people thought never mattered to them.'

'I didn't mean to offend you.'

'You didn't offend me. Honestly. It's the person we fall in love with, not the sex, not the gender and – forgive me – not the genitals either. It's not hard to understand . . . And, despite the perception, it's not about being greedy or promiscuous or any of that crude stereotyping that goes on.' He stops suddenly. He's over-explaining, sounding like he's confessing to some transgression that requires forgiveness.

She looks away, then back. 'Why are you telling me this?'

'I don't go around telling people this. Don't get me wrong, I don't conceal it either, but it's private and—'

'So why are you telling me?'

'I thought it was obvious . . . I like you. I thought it was mutual. Did I misread you?'

She shakes her head.

She cannot look him in the eye now. Poor girl. Hadn't expected this. Images crossing her mind. Aids victims, rent boys, saunas, glory holes, tops, bottoms . . . The pox. Jesus, she'll think I have it.

'Let's say I'm in a committed life-long relationship with a man,' he says, 'or in a committed life-long relationship with a woman – married to a woman, say, for twenty-five years. Well, what am I? Am I straight then? Or am I still regarded by the labellers as bisexual? How long would I have to be in a committed monogamous relationship with either a man or a woman to be regarded as either fully-fledged gay or fully-fledged straight? Do you see what I mean? How senseless labels are?'

She nods, looks out the window, then around at the room.

He came on too strong, too forceful. He does not want things to end this way.

'I should probably get going,' she says. She leaves her mug down and looks at him. 'I'll call you . . . And won't you let me know if Paddy is any trouble?'

His heart sinks. This is the way it will be, now and always, with women. Cannot put the genie back in the bottle. Must resign himself to men only.

He gets up and crosses the hearth and they stand facing each other. Without a word he leans in and kisses her on the mouth, and she lets him. Then he leads the way to the front door.

THE OLD PALL descends. He sleeps late. The cats gather at the front door, dishes pile in the sink. House of decay again, this.

He rises at noon, feeds the cats, lets Paddy out. He checks his phone incessantly, drinks strong coffee, smokes, watches Lynch's Friesians turn slowly towards the south. Turning and turning in the widening gyre. Stray bits of poems always dropping down. Feelings and sensations brought on by such lines. Moments that mattered most in his life. In his teenage years, in the back seat of the car, coming home from Cork on Saturday evenings. The car crawling out of the city, a book from the bookshop on Carey's Lane on his lap. Titles previously only heard of. *The Waste Land, Dubliners, Last Exit to Brooklyn.* Trying to read bits under the streetlights before the darkness of the countryside. Eyes on the words for the first time, joy and expectation surging up.

*   *   *

The week passes with no word from her. On Thursday he drives Ellen to Waterford for her eye clinic appointment and afterwards they have lunch at the Granville Hotel. When they have eaten she takes an envelope from her handbag and hands it to him.

'Instructions for my funeral,' she says. 'No unusual requests. No brass bands or gun salutes.'

He groans and takes the envelope. 'I won't be needing this for a long time, Ellen. Who knows who'll be buried first?'

'I'm not being morbid, you know,' she says. 'Just practical. I'm eighty-one years of age, Luke. The day can't be that far off. And I'm tired. Some days I think I've outstayed my welcome. At this stage I'm only biding my time. Hopefully, when the time comes I'll expire in my sleep, or nod off in my armchair watching CNN News. Obama's the last voice I hear as I go out.'

She'll be buried down at the end of the graveyard. She bought a double plot for herself and Josie when she came back from America, but then Josie went into the family grave with Dadda and his parents. Then Luke's mother joined them two years ago. That grave is bursting at the seams. Big expensive caskets. All the wood that's wasted. Bloom said they should bury people vertically – they'd fit more in if they put the coffins standing up.

'You're a mighty woman, Ellen O'Brien,' he says. 'You have a great attitude.'

'Ah, I don't know. Most people my age are down on their knees morning, noon and night praying for their salvation. I don't even go to Mass. God knows what's ahead of me!'

'Oh, you'll be all right. Sure all you ever did was good.'

'It's hard to know what to believe, isn't it? I don't know if there's a God or not, or a heaven or a hell . . . And I don't know which is worse – the possibility of an afterlife, or nothing at all. It might be better if there's nothing. But the thought of never seeing Mamma or Josie or your father . . . or Mrs Clark . . . ever again . . . I couldn't bear it.'

Her words catch him off guard. He lowers his head. All he can offer are platitudes, more platitudes. Better to be silent. Sit here with her. With her thoughts . . . Wonder what form we'll take then, if any. After our physical extinction. We might not go far. Might continue to exist in some other realm, some parallel universe maybe only inches from here. The soul close by . . . Don't know. There must be *something*. Some kind of energy operating in the universe. In all realms. Infinite realms. Wouldn't mind that. World without end.

'Did I see you out and about last week with a young lady at your side?' Ellen asks.

He is taken aback. She hasn't asked about his personal life in a long time. She had been fond of Maeve and sorry they broke up. What to say now. Five days and no word from Ruth. 'You did,' he says. You did indeed. A young lady.

'You're a good lad, Luke. You deserve to be happy. The next time she's around, come up and say hello. Just ring the bell, I'll be there.' She looks at him. 'If you feel like it, of course.'

*　　*　　*

In the evening he opens first a bottle of red wine and then the envelope with Ellen's funeral instructions.

1. *The open casket is to be placed in the living room (horizontal to the fireplace) for viewing. For easy flow of movement, people should enter from the hall and exit through the double doors into the dining room. NB: Cover the mirror.*

2. *Give the job to Feeney's Undertakers. Choose a light oak casket, like we had for Josie. Not those dark mahogany ones.*

3. *I'd like Maura Lynch to lay me out.*

4. *I'd like to be laid out in my navy bouclé suit, and the cream silk blouse with the bow. They're hanging together on a single hanger in the wardrobe in the guest bedroom.*

5. *Notify the Dept. of Social Welfare of my death so they can cancel my pension.*

6. *Please do not leave me in the church overnight. Bring me straight from the house for Requiem Mass, then on for burial.*

7. *Book the Sullane Valley Hotel for a full three-course meal after the burial. Guests to be treated to two drinks.*

8. *As you know, Aidan Farrell has the original will (and you have a copy). He'll know the right time to read it, but if Lucy comes home for the funeral, it can be read the day after my burial.*

Thank you, Luke, I'll <u>always</u> be grateful for all you've done for me, and for all you did for Josie too. With all my love, Ellen.

Floored, blindsided with sorrow now. As if she's already gone. Speaking from beyond the grave . . . Cannot imagine being without her. The backbone of the family since Dadda died. No, longer. And now . . . Only a matter of time. He will be truly alone then. For the first time.

He folds the pages and returns them to the envelope. He should leave instructions for his own funeral. What does it matter? Who will care? Just so long as I'm well dead before they bury me. Next stop Eternity Junction. Bloom was right – there should be some law to pierce the heart to make sure you're dead. Poor Bloom. No Papa, no Mama, no Rudy, and no Milly or Molly either, in a way. His mother's maiden name was Higgins. *Ellen* Higgins! Coincidence, remembering that now. Bloom was thinking of his mother during Paddy Dignam's funeral in Glasnevin. Not clear if she's buried there, don't think so . . . Bloom is always thinking about death. Because of Rudy. His father, too. Death in Ennis. Suicide . . . That hotel is still there. Looked it up online a while back. Still trading, imagine! The Queens Hotel. Church Street now named Abbey Street. Fine nineteenth-century building, wrought-iron balcony above the front door. Traditional signage. Óstán na Banríona. Interior a different story. Photographs of earlier times too. The Joyce connection given only a brief mention. Seems to specialise in hen parties now. Queens Nite Club. Customer reviews. *Excellent party for 32 hens. A lad called Ronnie looked after us* . . . Felt close to Bloom looking at the earlier pictures. Must go there sometime, ask for the room it happened in. Venetian blinds and hunting pictures on the wall. Sunlight coming in, the room stuffy. The boot-boy gave evidence at the inquest. They thought he was asleep. Rudolph Virag. Yellow streaks on his face. They must be used to Joyce fans . . . Wonder if they have a room named after him. The Rudolph V. Bloom suite. No. No market in suicide. Aconite he took. They should allow assisted suicide. Do it for animals, so why not? Have to go to Switzerland. Digitalis. No, *Dignitas*. Digitalis is a flower, foxglove . . . Aconite is a flower too, that's why I . . . No mention of where he's buried . . . Surprising Joyce never went in for cremation. Best solution all round. That theologian who wrote *The Imitation of Christ* was buried alive by accident; discovered the lid of his coffin gouged and clawed with his fingernails when they dug him up. Poor devil. Was up for sainthood but they wouldn't give it him – not saintly enough because he didn't willingly surrender to the will of God who had buried him alive.

On Saturday morning there is no sign of Lily. He calls and calls and finally she appears down the back stairs. She runs into the kitchen, tail in the air, her two sides beat together. Her litter has landed. She gobbles down her breakfast, then stands at the door, waiting for him. She leads the way up the back stairs and into the blue room. Hops into the wardrobe. Maternity ward. Five tiny, blind mewling kittens birthed on his mother's caramel coat. Marvel of nature. She steps daintily over them, folds herself down and lies back as they trample over each other to suckle. Such a good little mother. Worn out. This is your last little family, I promise, he whispers.

The doorbell rings. Startled, he runs to the window. Parked below, the little yellow car. His heart jumps and he races down the stairs, glancing at himself quickly as he passes the hall mirror. Then she's standing before him at the door.

'Ruth, come in.'

Paddy comes running from the yard and dives in the gap as the door is closing.

'Well, look at who it is!' she exclaims, bending down to pet him. 'Hope you're behaving yourself, buster.'

They make small talk about the dog. Then he says, 'I'm going to put him out now again, just for a little while. I've something to show you.'

He leads her up the back stairs and puts a finger to his lips before entering the blue room. Inside, he says Lily's name softly and opens the wardrobe door a fraction wider. Ruth squats down and looks inside.

'Oh . . . the little darlings,' she whispers. 'How many?'

He holds up five fingers.

She is trying to make them out in the semi-darkness. 'You're a great girl, Lily,' she whispers. Then she stands and moves back. 'I don't want to distress her.'

'I'm sorry for the silence all week,' she says.

They are sitting at the kitchen table.

He shrugs. 'No problem. I understand. And there was no obligation to speak.' She looks different. Younger. No mascara, that's the reason, her eyes are bare.

'The last day . . . you said you liked me,' she says.

'I did. I do.'

'I like you too, Luke. And . . .'

He waits. And is better than but. Then a thought strikes

103

him: what if she just wants to experience something exotic, a little deviant even? Wants to appear open-minded and evolved.

'I'd like to get to know you,' she says haltingly, then shrugs. 'I *want* to know you.'

'I want to know you too,' he says. 'But, you know, I'm not some curiosity, some experiment. And I'll never apologise for who I am.'

'I know that.'

They talk for an hour or more. She asks tentative, half-apologetic questions about his past. The who, when, where, how long? Not the what, or the who put what where. He wouldn't have answered anyway. Sacrosanct, always, the intimacy between two people.

'If, as a teenager, I had kissed a boy,' he says, 'and had never kissed a girl, then desire for *men only* might have been awoken in me, and I might never have been attracted to women . . . Until I met you, of course,' he teases. Need to lighten things up. 'Conventions, societal taboos – they prevent us from following desires that are completely natural. Why do we think desire can *only* be awoken in us by certain people, certain genders? How do we know?'

'You think it's that simple?' she asks. 'You're saying if I'd kissed a girl when I was fifteen I might now be a lesbian?'

'Maybe. Maybe not. Maybe you'd be attracted to both sexes . . . We're just people, Ruth. Not straight or gay or bisexual or trisexual. It's nobody's business who we're attracted to. It's a private matter between two people. Have you never been attracted to another woman?'

She smiles, gives a cheeky little look, makes a wavy maybe signal with her hand.

He opens his eyes wide in mock astonishment. 'Ah-ha!' he says. 'I feel an admission coming on.'

'Once – just once,' she says, 'at the airport en route to Paris, there was this girl in the queue behind me . . . It came out of nowhere. Honest to God! Our eyes met and she smiled at me. She was very beautiful, petite, brown-eyed, very French-looking, wearing a tight white shirt. I kept turning around – I couldn't take my eyes off her. She was very attractive. Sexually too.'

He keeps looking at her. 'And?' he says, signalling her to continue.

'That's it.'

'That's it? Ah, God, I thought you were about to confess to some act of wild abandon in public.'

'Fraid not. Wrong woman. I'm even mortified telling you that.'

He keeps his eyes on her. 'No need to be mortified.' He reaches across, takes her hand and kisses it.

She comes again the next day, dashing from the car to the front door in a downpour. A shy hug, lips brushing cheeks.

He lights a fire in the drawing room and they sit together on the sofa.

'When you asked me, that first day,' she says, 'if I had kids, I said no. And I don't. But I lost a child – a stillbirth – when I was married.'

He puts his arm around her shoulder and squeezes it. 'I'm sorry,' he says and he can feel her lean against him.

'It's okay, it's in the past. I'm not trying to elicit sympathy or anything. People have far worse stories than mine.'

'What happened?'

'We never knew. One of those things . . . It was a boy, full term. We had a little service in the chapel in the Coombe with just the two families. Then we drove across the city to Glasnevin. He's buried in the Angels' Plot there – they put ten or twelve little coffins in each grave, stacked on top of each other. I got a shock when we arrived. I thought he'd have his own little grave.'

He is shocked too. Bereaved parents, not knowing until they arrive. Too late then. He thinks of the little white coffins stacked up. A mass grave. Filling up each day. The husband leading her from the grave.

He kisses the top of her head. 'I'm very sorry you went through all that,' he whispers.

They are quiet for a while. Her hand is resting on his chest. She runs her fingers into the gap between two shirt buttons and touches his skin. He inhales deeply. Her fingers open a button, two buttons.

'What's this?' she asks. 'What happened?'

She is touching the thin pink skin of his scar.

'I had an argument with a bottle,' he says. 'The bottle won.'

She frowns. 'A fight?'

He shakes his head. 'I fell down drunk one night outside the Barge. I fell on my glass.'

She looks from his eyes to his scar and back again, the image forming in her mind. Falling down drunk. He can almost hear the clickety-click of her thoughts. He shouldn't have said that. She'll think . . .

'It sounds serious,' she says.

He shakes his head, looks away. 'Fairly superficial.' He does not say he ended up in St Vincent's A&E that night. The girl he was meeting for a second date – Sally Meehan – came with him in the ambulance. They lasted three or four months, held together by that fall.

She strokes the scar. 'The ancients thought that a scar was where the soul tried to leave the body,' she says, 'but the time wasn't right, so it had to squeeze back in again at the same spot. The person got a second chance.'

Nice little snapshot of the soul, he thinks, squeezing back in. Souls all around us, coming and going, ducking and diving. We don't know the half of it. *Soul is the form of forms.* Stephenspeak. Never understood that.

'A second chance,' he says. 'Mmm, I know a few souls that might have been better off escaping.'

She sits up, looks at him. Strangers can fall in love just by looking in each other's eyes. Don't have to say a word. Animosity wanes too. They did experiments – a Jew and a Muslim sitting across a table. Eventually they smiled.

Somewhere in the house the radio is on.

'This is lovely,' she says. 'Isn't this lovely?'

He touches her face, kisses her. 'It is.'

'Can we take it slowly?' she asks. 'For now, I mean. Can we not . . . you know? Is that okay?'

'Yes, of course,' he whispers. He takes a deep breath. The

smell of her. 'It's all okay. Anything you want or don't want is okay. All we have to be is honest. No games.'

From the radio, odd notes mingling, musical chaos. An orchestra tuning up, he thinks.

'I love those moments before a concert begins,' he whispers. 'When the orchestra warms up and the violinists lift their bows and they all take the key.' He tells her about a character in a novel who tries to convince his lover to make love in time with Schubert's String Quintet.

'You're not going to go all Schuberty on me, are you?' she asks.

He sinks his teeth lightly in her arm, closes his eyes. 'Forget Schubert,' he says. 'Look at us! Coming together like planets!'

In the evening, he shows her around the house, into every room. Afterwards they cook and carry the food up to the dining room.

She eyes the wall of books. 'Any update on poor Seamus Seoighe and the pox?'

'No change, I'm afraid. The subject may be dead and the symptoms dormant but the evidence prevails.'

She glances at the bookshelves. 'I wish I'd studied English. In your company I feel very *under* read. I've never read *Ulysses*, you know.'

'I'll read it to you. We'll read it together.'

'I'll hold you to that . . . Why are you so taken with Joyce, so devoted?'

Where to start. How to put it into words, this ache, this

longing for Joyce and Bloom both. Feels inseparable from Bloom. Consubstantial with . . . The two as one, creator and created: himthem. And grief for Joyce. The private afflictions, the deep suffering. No word for all this. Maybe in another language . . . German maybe, they're good at that . . . *Schadenfreude, Weltschmerz, Sehnsucht.*

'The work, obviously,' he says. 'The genius of it. Leopold Bloom especially.' The integrity of it. The commitment to the quotidian. His refusal to take conventions for granted. But why say what's always said? The banality of that. 'And the man himself, his humanity. His wit – he was a constant punster, a quipster. But he was also a very polite man, thoughtful, sensitive, reserved. People don't think of him in that way. And for all of his success and all his flaws – and he had many – I think of his life as sad and lonely.'

'But he had Nora.'

'He did. He had Nora.'

The image of Nora, ever constant, fills him with a gentle sorrow. The two of them, young and carnal together. Nora sitting in dark rooms for hours, looking from her. Decades of hardship, poverty, family woes. Threatening to leave. Not so carnal any more. He must have infected her. Hate to think that. Private. He must've been wracked with guilt and remorse. She'd have sensed it, women intuit these things . . . Lost without him in her final years.

'And George and Lucia,' he adds, 'and little Stephen. Family was everything to him.'

Suddenly, he is arrested by an image. December 1940, Joyce, Nora, George and eight-year-old Stephen, the flight out of France into Switzerland. Like the flight of the Holy Family out of Egypt. He looks at Ruth, about to tell her this. Joyce walking around the French village every day, heartsick, heartsore. Months of uncertainty, worry about Lucia. George cycling back and forth to Vichy to get permits and passports stamped. Cycling to Vichy again to buy a gallon of petrol for a car he'd hired to take them to the station for the 3 a.m. train. The little group huddled together on the platform with their belongings, scarcely speaking for fear of incrimination. Joyce with only twenty-eight days left to live. Did he know? Feel some portent? He who was always sensitive to harbingers and omens must have experienced a moment when everything was presciently clear. At the border, not enough money to pay the duty on Stephen's bike, so the bike was left behind and Stephen was promised a new one when they got to Zurich.

He is aware of the silence.

'It has been scientifically proven,' she says, 'that when we think of someone, there's a high probability that they too are thinking of us at that very moment.'

He thinks she means Joyce. That Joyce thinks of him when he thinks of Joyce and for a second he is thrown, and deeply moved by her understanding. But then as they look at each other it becomes clear. She is thinking not of Joyce, but of the two of them.

Soon she will leave. When she goes everything will change, the air will have a different density. He scours his mind for a means to detain her but already, in her own mind, she has left and is driving north through the country, waiting for the first sighting of the orange lights of the city up ahead on the horizon. He has to fight the urge to say *Take me with you.*

The beginning is beautiful. He is full to bursting with energy and every hour is happy. Alone, during the week, he tries to read but his mind weaves and wanders. He cleans the house from top to bottom, puts flowers on the mantelpiece, speaks kindly to the cats, even to the dog. 'Work with me, Paddy,' he pleads, 'and remember – you're still on probation.' At night, too wound to sleep, he re-lives their conversations. He remembers her lost child. Carried him for nine months. Almost full term. *Arrest of embryonic development at some stage antecedent to the human.* Bloom in Holles Street, the men rabbiting on with their embryological codology. Harelips and supernumerary digits and faceless foetuses and superstitions about pregnant women stepping over stiles. Women's lot is harder. The husband with her through it all. Buried a child together. No greater bond. He'd be what . . . six or seven now? The little funeral cortege crossed the city from the Coombe. Up to Glasnevin, like Paddy Dignam's funeral. He was still teaching in Belvedere then. It might have passed him on the street, going up along Parnell Square. Grief-ferrying cars. Everyone outside oblivious. The husband driving, the tiny coffin on her lap. She must think of him, even now. Bloom was always thinking of little Rudy . . . in an Eton suit, a little lamb in his pocket. If he'd lived, helping him on in life. Tipped the gardener to keep his grave free of weeds. *My son.* Conceived one morning, Molly looking out the window at two dogs going at it. Give us a touch, Poldy. God, I'm dying for it. How life begins.

She comes again at the weekend. She startles him by just being there. They walk through the land and along the road by the river. He takes her hand. He wants to know everything, to be joined in the same neural rush.

She talks about her work; she tells him about a boy, Shane, whose mother abandoned him.

'He was raised by his grandmother,' she says, 'but he's in foster care now. The grandmother beat him every day since he was a baby. Do you know what she told me? She said, "He was bad since the day he was born." Those were her exact words.'

He has an image of her sitting across a table at a case conference or giving evidence in the children's court, dressed in a dark suit and court shoes, her legs in flesh-coloured tights.

He tells her of his childhood summers, Ellen home from America, his father, mother, Lucy, the house full to the brim with activity. He tells about Una falling down the well, and about Josie, his heart's darling.

'Mammy and Lucy used to make fun of her — setting silly traps for her, laughing behind her back.' A form of gaslighting, now that he thinks about it. 'Look, Josie . . . is that Mike Baldwin? they'd say. She didn't understand TV — she thought everything on TV was real so when she'd see an actor from *Coronation Street* in another role – on another show – she'd be all confused, all put out. What's Mike Baldwin doing there? she'd say, he's supposed to be gone away with Alma this weekend. Mammy and Lucy could be right bitches to her at times . . . Nowadays,' he says, 'she'd be labelled special needs. She was more herself than any of us . . . She was actually a Buddhist without knowing it . . . She saw everything, but not the way we do. "Why is that flower there?" she'd ask. I'm not religious but she could touch the Kingdom of Heaven. Honest to God, that's how I think of her now. She had strange capacities, powers almost. She *saw* the flower and *knew* the flower. It's hard to explain. No explanations of science or psychology or anything rational can explain all she understood.'

They cross a ditch into his field. Lynch's cows stop grazing to look at them. He notices clay stuck to her shoes. She will carry the clay back to the city, he thinks, and in that instant he is filled with hope.

'You know what you told me earlier about losing the child?' he says. 'Is it okay to ask about—?'

'Yes, of course.'

'Did you and your husband not try again?'

She shakes her head. 'Things were difficult – they'd been getting difficult even before we lost the child. Paul was – is – French. He's a sommelier – he worked at Patrick Guilbaud's. He lives in New York now . . . He's very successful but it's a stressful life, with very long hours.' She looks at Luke. 'He was drinking too much.' She shrugs. 'And doing cocaine too. They live hard fast lives in that world. Anyway, he and I were never a good fit. During the pregnancy I had this constant vague fear – a feeling of impending doom. An intuition, I suppose. I could never *visualise* us as a family. It all seemed surreal, like a dream, and I never felt the child was real or that a child would be born . . . I know that sounds odd, and I've never said this to anyone before, or even articulated it for myself. It was a premonition. As if the child wasn't . . . *deemed.*' She stops and grows pensive. 'I don't think we would have made a good family. The time wasn't right and the chemistry wasn't right. Even the biology, when you think of it, didn't work.'

A child not deemed. We are alike. She thinks like me.

She gives a little laugh. 'I just remembered something! My obstetrician was a short, fat, bald, middle-aged man – Paul called him Dr DeVito. In the weeks after it all happened, I felt close to Dr DeVito, closer to him than to Paul. I felt safe with him – it's not uncommon after a trauma. People feel a bond with their doctors. Anyway, at one point – don't laugh – I actually fantasised about *him* impregnating me – Dr DeVito! I thought if only he . . . then it would surely work!'

Cannot picture her pregnant, full with child. See heavily pregnant women with their men on the street. Potent image. The bigger, the better. The men know it too. *This is what I did to her, I filled her up, gave her this big belly.* Leave the rest to the imagination . . . Bloom in Nighttown peeping through the keyhole at Blazes Boylan and Molly. *Plough her. More. Shoot!* The lustier they are, the better. Better chance it'll take. Fecundity of the compatible.

* * *

114

They go away to a beautiful hotel by the sea in Kinsale. They stay awake most of the night, talking, their heads on one pillow. On Sunday morning, church bells ring out across the town into their room. His hand is resting on her thigh. She lifts her head and kisses him.

'Do you have condoms?' she asks.

He nods, kisses her eyes, her mouth, her breasts, the faint stretch marks on her belly. Nervous, fearful of hurting her, he enters her gently, then remains very still. It is, he thinks, like he has been airlifted from one country and set down in another.

'What are you thinking about?' she asks afterwards.

'How happy I am,' he replies.

'Liar.'

Little emanations of the word carry in the air, rising and falling in subtle little movements of sound. A harsh word, liar, but spoken now without harshness.

'Go on, tell the truth. What were you thinking?' she asks.

He smiles. '*A stout shield of oxengut*,' he says. 'That's what the boyos in *Ulysses* call a condom, or what served as a condom in those days!'

'Ugh, oxengut . . . disgusting!'

'And you?' he asks gently. 'What were you thinking?'

She waits for a few moments. 'You. Your past. Your gay past.'

He closes his eyes, inhales. Does she have to? Ruin the moment. Ruin everything.

He sits up. 'Please don't say that.'

'How do you know you won't go back to men?' she asks. 'How do I know?'

'How do *I* know *you* won't go back to men? To other men, to your husband?'

'That's different.'

'How is it different? If someone is going to leave or be unfaithful, it doesn't matter who they're unfaithful with . . . I told you: I'm one hundred per cent monogamous. That's the only question – whether one is monogamous or not.'

Tonight I am reading Borges, he writes in an email. 'The angels are two days and two nights older than we: the Lord created them on the fourth day, and from their high balcony between the recently invented sun and the first moon they scanned the infant earth.'

Do you love that as much as I do? How come only the angels have survived? How come we've no devils or dragons or werewolves or unicorns any more – except in fantasy? No serpents or centaurs or phoenixes either.

Borges moves me – his shyness, his gentleness. I feel his loss, a bit like Joyce's. I mean the loss of him to the world. He called his mother Madre, and she called him Georgie. They lived gently together. He lived very simply, ate only plain food. I want to be more like that. I'm going to give up meat. I want to live simply and honestly.

'The question is not can they reason, or can they talk, but can they suffer?' she writes. I came across that quote when I was seventeen. When I moved to Dublin I went to talks on animal rights. Tom Regan, an American philosopher, came to Trinity once. I fell in love with him, I read everything he wrote. The rights of the weak and the voiceless trump ours, he says. I read Peter Singer and Andrew Linzey, all the philosophy and science and the animal theology I could get my hands on, and I read all about the animal experiments too. I thought about becoming a Jain – the mercy they feel for every living thing makes me ashamed of how little I do. Do you know the Jains won't walk through a puddle because of the microbes, they don't eat root vegetables because digging them up endangers worms and upsets the subterranean ecosystem. In those days all I thought about were animals: their mute lives, their everyday realities, minute by minute. I'd lie awake at night haunted by some photograph or memory – a lame horse I'd spotted that day, or a hunt I'd met on the road, or a photograph of a laboratory monkey having its eyes sewn up. I was obsessed, consumed, on the verge of a breakdown.

I had to tamp it all down. Now I think of myself as weak and cowardly for not speaking up more, for being so afraid.

I don't want to be afraid any more. I want to be free. You're free. I never met anyone so free. You don't care what people think. And yet there's something old-fashioned about you – do you mind me saying this? You're a curious mix of modern and traditional. What twenty-something-year-old man would take six months off work to mind his sick aunt? I love that about you – your conviction to do what's right, no matter what. xr

I love writing to you! I want to write to you all day! Today I made a To Do list. Item No. 1: Ulysses with Ruth. We'll start this weekend – I cannot wait! Thus inspired, I took down Finnegans Wake. It's a nightmare, but I'm determined to get a handle on it. I started underlining all the intelligible sentences and clauses I came upon. I could hear Nora everywhere. 'I done me best when I was let . . . But you're changing, acoolsha, you're changing from me, I can feel. Or is it me?' I'm going to type them all up so we can read them aloud together. I don't know if Joyce would be amused or appalled but we'll have such fun! Lx

P.S. Attached is a pic of a lewd drawing from the flyleaf of my FW. The artwork is not mine. This (defaced) copy of FW is, I'm ashamed to admit, one I borrowed from UCD's library sometime in 1999 and never returned. Don't judge me too harshly – this, a bar of Aero when I was 11 and a fiver from my mother's handbag when I was 15, are the only things I've ever stolen.

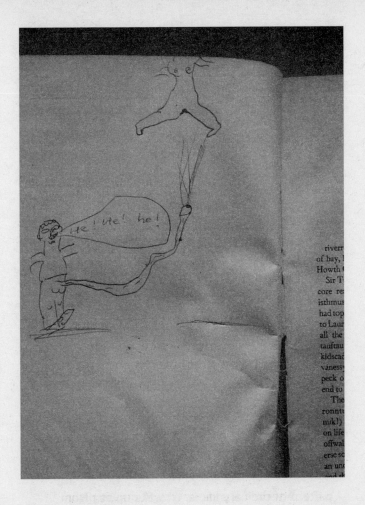

You durty thief you!

I love writing to you, too. I have imaginary conversations with you all the time. And every hour something seems to drop into my lap that I want to share
with you. Today I read about scientists in
Massachusetts who have grown human heart tissue
inside a spinach leaf. At lunch one day, one of the

119

scientists looked at a spinach leaf on his plate and was reminded of an aorta. They discovered that the network of veins in a spinach leaf replicates exactly the micro vascular system in the human heart. I nearly cried when I read that. They flushed out the veins in some spinach leaves with detergent, stripping them of their green plant cells, and then filled them with human heart tissue.

After five days, the muscle cells began to pulse.

xr

Josie lost her childhood when Una fell down the well, he writes, but she got it back with Lucy and me. I'm going to marry Lukey, she'd say, and then run to fetch the broom and lay it on the ground between us for the mock wedding. All her life she drank her tea from a saucer. She kept nests of kittens in her room. She ate chocolate muffins in bed at night. She could probably hear our hair growing.

I was bereft when she died. I thought: how easy it is to die, how fragile and easily extinguished the pattern of ordinary life is. I'd wake up at night shaking and frightened. Some days I couldn't breathe for her loss, my arms liquid with love for her. And then one night, I felt myself rise from the bed, and hover, and observe myself from above. I started to interrogate that self that lay on the bed. It was like an inquisition, but what accrued slowly was a record of my life and with it a validation of me. I was no longer afraid. Even as it was happening, even as I was looking down and interrogating myself, I knew it was the machinery of my mind restoring order on a shocked, bereaved self.

Why, in the larger picture, she even existed? But people as good as Josie calibrate those around them. Humans are moved by rivers and mountains. She could implore something beautiful down from the sky into her apron. Pigeons descended to be close to her. As if she herself had been in the sky. As if she, in all her simplicity, had more answers than God. But of course she and simplicity had nothing in common. She was deeper and more damaged than any of us. But she was safe with me.

Lx

Shane, the boy I told you about, is in a secure unit in Oberstown tonight. The foster parents sent him back. He had a pillow-fight with the eleven-year-old boy in the family. He'd snuck a brick into his pillow before-hand. And the thing was, he actually liked this family. They were his best chance, maybe his last chance. xr

I want to meet your mother and your sisters, and I want you to meet Ellen. She's like a mother to me. I wish you'd known Josie, and my mother and father.

Write to me, Ruth. Write to me honestly. Tell me everything. 'Love is unhappy when love is away.' Lx

Be honest, you say . . . Well, late at night I'm plagued by thoughts of your past. You, with men. I feel very unevolved saying this. I tell myself these fears will subside. I keep thinking: why did you suddenly change direction, sexually, when you were twenty-seven? You must have had an inkling before then, felt the change coming. In the dead of night all these fears rain down on me – I'm convinced, for instance, that you share some secret bond with every man you meet, and that being with me will deprive you of something. Will it? Will a part of you always be unreachable to me? Please be patient with me. It's not love if it's not jealous – I don't believe anyone who says otherwise. xr

ONE SUNDAY AFTERNOON, when they are out for a walk, they visit Ellen.

'We won't stay long,' Luke says after he has introduced Ruth and Ellen to each other. 'Ruth is heading back to Dublin shortly.'

'Your house is lovely,' Ruth says. She is sitting on the edge of the sofa, her feet tucked in under her.

He watches Ellen watching Ruth. Sizing her up. Guessing her age. Women can be hard on each other. Ellen wanting only what's good for him, but maybe no woman will ever be good enough for him, or for Ardboe. Used to call Mammy Her Ladyship when she was irked.

'And the garden too,' Ruth says. 'You have a great view.'

Ellen turns towards the window and in the second her head is turned Luke catches Ruth's eye and gives her the briefest wink and then, barely stirring a muscle, makes a swift, furtive thumbs-up sign from hands resting calmly on his thighs.

They talk a little about the garden. Ruth's mother likes

to garden, she says. Ellen is paying full attention. When she excuses herself and goes to the kitchen to make tea they are, in her absence, like giddy kids – whispering, poking each other, making faces.

When she returns with tea and biscuits she gives them a wide-eyed smile, as if surprised to find them still there.

'It was Ruth who got me the dog,' Luke explains.

'That's right, I remember. A nice little fella – by the look of him,' Ellen says. Then, turning to Ruth, 'Luke is a big softie when it comes to animals.'

'Oh, she's much worse herself,' he says, nodding towards Ruth. 'I'm only in the halfpenny place compared to her.'

They drink the tea. For a while the only sound is the little tinkle of china when they leave the cups down. Luke's foot starts tapping. Lost for words, all of them.

He hops up and takes down a framed photograph from the mantelpiece. 'That's Ellen there,' he says, pointing, 'with the family she worked for in America . . . Wasn't she a fine-looking woman in her day?'

Ruth scans the photo and looks at Ellen. 'Luke told me you lived in America for years.'

'I did indeed. Forty-two years. I went there when I was twenty-three.'

'It must've been a big change coming back after all that time. You must miss America.'

Ellen hesitates, as if thrown by the question. 'I'm back a long time now,' she says. 'Sixteen years. I miss certain things – the variety of foods, the weather in springtime, everywhere so clean and tidy, especially on Long Island

124

where I lived.' She gives a little laugh. 'The mailboxes too
– familiar things . . . the front lawns, even the yellow school
buses.' She pauses and looks at Ruth. 'America was very good
to me for all those years.'

She offers more tea. 'I always knew I'd come back though,'
she continues. 'I thought I'd come back when I was still
young, and settle down here.'

He has the sense that she is trying to tell him something.
Tell *them*. That life is short, perhaps.

Ruth is still gazing at the photograph.

'That was taken out in California,' Ellen says, leaning over
a little to look at it. 'Around 1973 or '74, I think. We're all
there at the ranch, sitting around on the terrace. Mrs Clark
moved out there permanently a few years later.'

'They were very wealthy, the Clarks, weren't they, Ellen?'
Luke says. 'Ellen did everything and went everywhere with
them – she'd be called a personal assistant today. Mrs Clark's
brother was a politician – the Governor of Vermont, was
it, Ellen?'

She nods. 'It was a good life.'

Ruth hands him the photo and gives him a look he
cannot interpret. All the ways to read each other still
unknown.

'I think Luke said you're from Dublin, Ruth?' Ellen says.

'No, I'm from just a few miles out the road, Curraboy.
I work in Dublin all right.'

'What did you say your name is?'

'Ruth, Ruth Mulvey. My mother's name is Angela. Maybe
you know her?'

Ellen nods. 'I don't know your mother personally, I only know of her.'

After a few moments, he says, 'We'd better head off soon. Ruth has to drive back to Dublin.'

At the door, the two women shake hands. Luke hugs Ellen. 'I'll give you a call later,' he says quietly. When he goes to draw away, she holds onto him for a moment longer than he expects.

'There's no need to call me later,' she says. 'Drop up to me in the morning, will you? I want to talk to you.'

He looks at her curiously. 'Sure. Are you okay?'

'Yes,' she says and taps him lightly on the back, a little there-there tap. 'Off you go, now.'

'DID YOU KNOW?'

'Did I know what? . . . Ellen, what's wrong?'

They are in her sitting room the next morning. Her eyes are fixed on him.

'Is she Mossie Mulvey's daughter? Is that who she is?'

He makes a face. 'Who's Mossie Mulvey?'

She turns her head to the window.

'Ellen, please, what's going on? You're frightening me now.'

'What's her father's name?'

'Ruth's father is dead. Maurice, I think . . . yes, Maurice. What's Ruth got to—'

'That's him . . . Maurice. Mossie Mulvey.' She looks him directly in the eye. 'You have to give her up.'

'*What?*'

'She's bad news, Luke. Give her up.'

'What are you talking about, Ellen? What's gotten into you?'

'I was engaged to her father years ago. It ended badly. I had to take him to court.'

His stomach lurches.

'You know those big trunks of mine above in the house? There's a wedding gown in one of them. It was bought in Bloomingdales in New York one morning in the autumn of 1962. Mrs Clark was with me – it was her gift to me. It cost $450, an absolute fortune at the time . . . I never got to wear it.'

He is shaking his head. 'Stop, please. Slow down. What happened?'

'I was a fool, that's what happened. I made the mistake of thinking that Mossie Mulvey was a good, honest man. He *seemed* honest. He had a fine farm, he came from a good family. We were a good match – and that mattered in those days. And, much as I loved the Clarks, I never wanted to stay in America. I was always going to come home and settle down.'

'What happened? What went wrong?'

'He lied, that's what went wrong! Why, I'll never know. We got engaged in the summer of '62 and planned to marry the following summer when I'd move back home for good. But a few months after I returned to the States – after getting engaged – he started to pull away from me. In his letters, I mean. The letters became less warm and less frequent. Oh, I should have confronted him – I know that now. But at the time I was afraid – afraid to admit that anything might be wrong. So I ploughed on with the plans, bought my wedding gown, my wedding chest, all that stuff.'

A fly lands on a paper napkin on the coffee table beside him. It seems to be moving its forelegs, like hands, over its head, like a cat washing.

'I'd write him letters telling him how I couldn't wait to be married,' she says, 'telling him how much I missed him and . . . loved him. I'd be longing for his letters – they were our only means of communication. But his were getting scarcer and more distant and finally I asked him straight out if everything was okay, or if I had done or said anything to offend him. Well, he hummed and hawed and avoided answering that question for weeks. Then he said yes, I had annoyed him a few times when I was home . . . He made out that I told him *what to do*, and that what I said and the way I said it sounded to him like an order! Well, I was mortified. I apologised profusely, explaining I never meant to sound like that, that I only wanted what was best for him. Anyway, that wasn't really it, that was just a cover, that was him trying to set things up.'

Luke's heart is thumping. 'Go on,' he says. 'What happened?'

'He claimed to have received anonymous letters about me . . . saying nasty things about me. He said he got three or four of these letters over several months. Well, I was stunned. I couldn't believe it – who would write nasty letters about me? I had no enemies here – or anywhere.'

'But who would – I don't understand.' He shakes his head. 'It makes no sense.'

She is silent, looking at him.

'Ellen?'

'Are you're doubting me, Luke?'

'Go on, Ellen, please. Tell me what happened.'

She takes off her glasses, rubs her eyes. 'Before any of

this trouble . . . before it all went wrong, there were good times – normal, happy times, Luke. I want you to know that. Dancing, little road trips, boat rides on the river . . .'

She takes a deep breath. 'What I'm trying to say is that there *was* a relationship, a real relationship between Mossie and me. Your father knew him. We'd all go to the dances together and they'd talk about cattle and the beet harvest and things . . . It existed, it was not some figment of my imagination.'

'But why? Who would do such a thing?'

'I don't know. I'll never know why any of it happened. I told him over and over that there was no truth in those letters, that it was all malicious lies. I begged him to ignore them or at least go to the Guards. At that stage my main concern was to reassure *him* that I was telling the truth . . . It was a terrible time, Luke, and . . . also, I felt for him too, you know, I really did. It was tough being so far away from him, every day waiting for a letter from him and nearly always being disappointed. Sleepless nights, worrying constantly, thinking that all this would reach Mamma and upset her.'

She shakes her head. 'I wrote *every* day pleading with him to believe me. I'd dash down to the post office in Laurel Hollow at lunchtime to get a letter out in the afternoon post. Begging him constantly to stay strong and believe me, and that when I got home we'd get to the bottom of this together.'

She looks at Luke. 'I was going up the wall – being so far from him, not able to talk to him. We arranged a few phone calls but he wasn't much good on the phone . . . and nothing I said seemed to reassure him. And that made me even lonelier and more frightened.'

Silence again, the image of the phone calls lingering. His heart racing.

'What was in the letters, what sort of lies?'

'Does it matter, at this stage?'

'It does.'

She averts her eyes and sighs.

'He said the letters were warning him about me, tipping him off. He said they claimed that I had a child in America, that I was "a loose woman" . . . A loose woman!' She lets out a wry, bitter little laugh. 'Someone – or someone who knew someone – had a baby in a hospital in New York a few years before, and apparently I was in the bed next to her, after giving birth! Can you credit it!'

'And were there letters? Did you actually see them?'

'Eventually he produced two. I believe he wrote them himself, or got a drinking pal to write them.'

He brings a hand to his face.

'The correspondence went on like this, back and forth between us for months,' she continues. 'I was going out of my mind. I never expected for one minute that he'd doubt me. Not for one minute! It was awful, awful . . . Going to bed every night after a long day's work, full of fear and dread, waking up to face another day the same way. Finally I wrote to your father and told him everything. Not an easy letter to write, as you can imagine. Your father met him and tried to get to the bottom of things but only came to a dead end. Eventually we had to tell Mamma. I came home early that summer, still hopeful I could sort things out – that once he saw me and heard the truth in person – out of my mouth – he'd have no doubts whatsoever. How wrong I was!

'I asked him to come up to Ardboe that first night, and he did, but he wouldn't come in. He waited in the car until Mamma and Josie and your father were gone to bed. Then he came into the kitchen, sheepish, you know. Everything was so fragile between us . . . I feel sick even now thinking of it . . . Answer me, yes or no, I said, do you believe what was written about me in those letters? I don't know, he said, it leaves a doubt. You either believe them or you don't, I said, so which is it? I don't know, he said, I don't feel right inside, the letters are after coming between us. There was a long silence then. I remember thinking that he's a good man and I'm a good woman and this – this shouldn't be happening, and if we stick at it and if we have good intentions, we'll be all right. And I really believed that. I felt this great peace coming over me and I reached out a hand to him, hoping he'd . . . But he didn't move. He just sat there like a stone. Finally I asked if he'd stand by me until I was either proven innocent or guilty. He couldn't even look at me. He shook his head. I don't feel right, he said, I think it's best to call things off . . . I remember the clock ticking behind me on the wall. It must have been past midnight by then. I could feel everything slipping away from me. I looked out the window into the night. I knew in my heart it was all over then.'

The clock on the wall. Not the same clock. The table is the same.

'They were terrible times, Luke, terrible times! Do you know what it was like for a woman to be labelled *loose* then? I knew it would be the end of me – no one would ever touch me. And all lies, *all lies* . . . But mud sticks, Luke, and especially to women. People love gossip and scandal and the more salacious the better. The whole parish was talking about me. The *unfairness* of it – it still rankles. Never really knowing if I was believed – because it's a man's world and women are the first to be doubted, women are never really trusted. I learned that lesson – how quick people are to malign women, view us as liars, as conniving. Even my own family, good as they were, I often wondered if they doubted me too. Mamma and your father – if they had moments when they thought, well, she's beyond in America and she might well have had a child and we wouldn't know. Don't tell me that thought didn't cross their minds. I had to do something! I was raging and frightened out of my wits – and grieving him too, and grieving all that was lost. But I had to clear my name and my reputation. I was *not* going to lie down under his damn lies. Never! I'm an O'Brien, Luke, and when it comes to the truth, I'm a lioness. So I consulted a solicitor – your father came with me to Cork – and the solicitor told me the best way to proceed was to sue Mossie for breach of promise and defamation. And that's what I did. But the upset it caused, the scandal! I thought it would all happen quickly but it dragged on for a couple of years, as these things do, back and forth between

133

the two solicitors, with all the usual delays and adjournments. Luckily I had kept all his letters – and he had kept mine. The case was originally to be heard in the Circuit Court in Cork, but because of the amount of damages we were looking for, we got it transferred to the High Court in Dublin.'

She pauses and looks at him. 'This happened, Luke, this really happened to me. Then, a short while before it was due to go to trial, I got a letter from him out of the blue. Offering to marry me! Can you imagine? It was a ploy. He wanted to avoid costs – that was his only motive, because at that stage he knew well he'd lose the case . . . What kind of man would . . .? What kind of marriage would that have been?'

She looks into his eyes, pleading. Must he answer her? Is she waiting?

'What happened?' he asks. 'In court? Was he found guilty?'

'We settled out of court on the morning. So there was no verdict, no guilty verdict. I often regret settling, I wish I'd had my day in court, but at the time I was terrified . . . and the pressure, the fear. It was horrendous! He was forced to admit he was wrong – that was the word that was used, *wrong*. He had to issue a formal apology for the charges and imputations he had made against me and my character. The apology was published in all the newspapers in the following days. And he had to pay me damages and pay my costs. So in the end, my reputation and good name were restored. But the lengths I had to go to – to prove . . .' She stops and looks away.

'It was a bittersweet victory, Luke, because the damage was done. And then, to top it all, the judge made a comment afterwards that took the good out of it. He said that the person who wrote the anonymous letters was responsible for a lot of the hurt and damage caused. That comment made Mossie look like a victim too. And that angered me, and still angers me, because he was no victim, I can tell you, and those letters were not anonymous. He set the whole thing up, I'm certain of it. I regret not hiring a handwriting expert to examine them – my solicitors slipped up there. But this was 1965 and I don't know if such a person even existed in Ireland at the time . . .'

She pauses. 'That's it, really. And then every summer after that – during all those years when I'd be home, I'd have to watch him parading up the aisle at Mass every Sunday with his wife and kids.'

Her voice is breaking. 'It was like a knife going through me. After Mamma died, I stopped going to Mass. Of course he went outside the parish – outside the county, in fact – for the new wife. A hard, swarthy little woman with a thin mouth. He didn't delay either – he was married within the year. I often wondered if she knew. But you'd have to know a thing like that. You'd sense it – you'd feel it off someone that close to you, wouldn't you Luke? . . . Marching up to Communion every single Sunday. Not a bother on him. Neck to burn!'

A wife. Children. Three daughters. Ellen watching them. Watching Ruth.

'How come I never knew this, Ellen?' His voice is weak.

He clears his throat. 'I don't understand. All these years, how come I never knew? How is that possible? . . . I knew you were engaged once but not this. I never knew anything about a court case. I can't believe Mam never told me, or I never heard rumours.'

'It was a long time ago and it was a great scandal. It happened years before your father and mother even met — ten years or more. It had all died down by the time your mother arrived here. And your mother was never one to pry or gossip. No one wanted to talk about it, Luke. We all wanted to put it behind us. It was a very painful chapter in our lives. And the neighbours were very kind and considerate . . . It all felt like, I don't know — a derailment — certainly in my life, but for the whole family too, and maybe even for the town. Poor Mamma, it almost killed her. Can you imagine how I felt bringing all this trouble down on top of the family? Your father was wonderful. I couldn't have gone to court without his support. It was tough on him, very tough on him in the years after that too, meeting Mossie around the town and at the mart.'

'But *why*? I don't understand. Why did he do it? It makes no sense.'

'I don't know, Luke. I'll never know. It could simply be that he got cold feet, that he lost his nerve and wanted to back out of the engagement but didn't have the courage to say it and, I don't know, maybe he panicked. That's the kindest way of looking at it. Or maybe he didn't feel he was good enough for me. Maybe *I* was at fault. I've had years to think about all this, Luke. Maybe *I* made him feel small somehow – with all my talk of America and the Clarks and the Governor of Vermont, the high life I appeared to be living. But the truth is, I don't know. I don't know what got into him. He went from being warm and kind in his letters, telling me every little thing he was doing on the farm, to being cold and distant, a different man. I quizzed him, thinking maybe he'd met someone else – another woman – but I don't think that was it . . . In the end, maybe it was for the best. Maybe I had a lucky escape. But do you know what kills me now? When I look back, he wasn't even that great a catch. Oh, he thought he was, like so many men at the time, thinking they were God's gift to women – and we women should be grateful. Grateful! When I think of the Clarks and all the cultured people I met in America – refined people, educated people! What was he but a small uneducated farmer?'

As she talks, a strange bodily sensation surfaces in him; a tingling, like a mild electric current, shoots down his left arm from his neck and spine. He inhales slowly, exhales, moves his eyes to the fireplace and lets them rest on the companion set. Tongs, shovel, brush, poker. The current is stronger now, more intense, the tingle spreading into his left hand, strengthening. Throbbing painfully through the fingers, rendering the whole hand numb and weak and inert, but thronged with current. He focuses on his left hand, lifts it slowly and leaves it gently in the palm of his right hand. Calmer now. Hand on hand. What a weak and pitiful thing a hand is.

'Last night, after your visit with . . . *her*, I was all up in a terrible state, thinking it *couldn't* be her, that I must be mistaken, this couldn't be happening! Of all the girls in the county, in the country . . .' She shakes her head. 'When I went to bed, I tossed and turned for ages. Then I got up and took down all the boxes of stuff I have down there in the spare room – his letters, all the solicitors' letters and documents – and I sorted through them. I was up all night.' She points to a plastic bag on the floor near the door. 'They're all there in that bag, the letters and the legal files. I want you to have them.'

He looks at the bag. He feels ill. 'Why? Why would I want them?'

'In case you ever doubt me.'

They stare at each other. He turns away and rubs his face. Ruth is at work now. Monday morning, at her desk, in her office on the North Strand. Or in Oberstown, visiting that boy.

'Why are you telling me this now, Ellen? What good will it do?'

'You are family, Luke. You are blood.' She looks at him, imploring. 'You need to know who you're associating with.'

'Who I'm *associating with* . . .? Who I'm *associating with*, Ellen! What kind of language is that? Are you an O'Brien at all, using that kind of language?'

She gives him a cold look. 'She's bad news, Luke. The apple doesn't fall far from the tree. You have to give her up.'

'Listen to yourself, Ellen! Ruth has nothing to do with what happened – Ruth did nothing.'

'Don't say her name again. I don't ever want to hear that name.'

He stares hard at her. 'You know what? Mam was right.' His voice starts to crack. 'You're just a meddler, Ellen, you're just a jealous old woman who cannot bear to see others happy.'

'Say what you like. But the truth is, I wanted you to be happy. When I saw you out and about and realised you'd met someone, I was looking forward to meeting her. I imagined having ye here for Sunday lunch. I want to see you settled down, and the house alive again.'

He shakes his head.

'Do you know what I went through, Luke? You have no idea, do you? . . . I had to be examined!'

He closes his eyes. He cannot bear much more.

'I will die soon enough, Luke,' she says, leaning towards him, 'but you . . . you have your whole life before you. This — *this woman* — there's bad blood there, Luke, *bad blood*. You might not see it now but, believe me, bad blood will show itself, it's the nature of the beast. Nature always wins out in the end.'

'Stop . . . *Please.*'

She turns towards the window. He follows her gaze to a robin hopping along the windowsill in tender little hops. The bird pauses, then turns and hops back the way he came.

'Luke, how long do you know this woman? A month? Two months?'

He shrugs.

'How long?'

'A month.'

'A month . . . Thirty days. And how well do you know

her? *Really* know her? What is she like when she gets upset, or angry? Think about that. Thirty days. Walk away now, Luke, while it's still easy. You won't regret it.'

He shakes his head, tears stinging his eyes.

'Oh, I know it's hard. I know it is. And I hate to see you cry. But you'll shed a lot more tears if you continue with her. Give her up . . . If you won't do it for my sake, then do it for your father's, a man who never put a foot wrong or spoke an ill word about anyone in his life. And for your mother's too – for all our differences she was family to me.'

'You can't just drag something up from fifty years ago, Ellen, and hit me with it, dump it on me! Just when I'm happy . . . You can't do this, you can't.'

'I didn't drag anything up, Luke. I didn't ask for this, any more than you did. Do you think I want the past – and all that pain – erupting in my life again?'

'It's not Ruth's fault, Ellen. Why should she be punished? Why should I be punished?'

'If you keep with that lady, Luke, you'll regret it. Mark my words, you'll rue the day you ever met her.'

'I can't believe what you're saying, Ellen. You're acting as judge and jury over an innocent woman, condemning her. Shame on you!'

'Fine. Please yourself. Make your bed. Lie on it. But I'll lay it out fair and square for you now.' She looks him in the eye. 'If you bring that woman into Ardboe, if you bring her into that house and parade her around here and humiliate me – *deliberately* humiliate me – that's it, I won't leave you a penny. Lucy will get everything – this house and the

140

money too. You won't get a red cent. I'll get the hackney into Cork in the morning and change my will.'

'Keep your money, Ellen. I don't care about your fucking money.' He stands up.

'Oh, you care!'

She struggles to rise.

He makes for the door, savage in his stride.

'Go on, off with you!' she says, reaching for the plastic bag on the floor. 'And take these with you.'

He stops, dazed, in the doorway. She shoves the bag into his arms and he does not resist.

'They're all there,' she says, 'the letters, the files, everything. You might even find the receipt for the wedding dress. She might get the wear out of it yet – that'd be a nice how-do-you-do for this family!'

HE SEES HIMSELF, as if from above, moving slowly down the drive. He feels himself, as if from above; his heart pounding, his head throbbing, his mouth dry. His stomach in spasm. His ears thronged with the *pick-pack-pock-puck* of his boots on the tarmac. The sky above — above the above — ready to cleave asunder. Coffined thoughts surround him. No more aunt. No more Ellen. His molecules shuttle to and fro. The hole in his right sock releases the big-toe lady at last. Gibberish thoughts, fatuous images. *Ride a cockhorse to Curraboy Cross.* Oh, but you'll rue the day, mark my words, my rue, rue, ruthless ruth . . . Thirty days! My ver, ver, virgin aunt. Up we go, hup-hup, good girl, open wide.

Something moves. Where? On the road. *Keep in, keep in.* What now? No more Ruth. What now? Discern. Let the mind discern. Let the feet walk. Let the heart becalm itself . . . *Tharump, tharump, tharump.*

What happened?

The worst thing.

What now?
Unable to say.
Unable to say what?
Unable to say *I* . . . No more I.

AS HE TURNS in the avenue what images, prompted by the licking of hot salty tears, come to mind?

Pillars. Lot's wife. His brain in disarray. His brain on the verge of a cataplectic fit caused by the autoimmune destruction of neurons as he tries to fathom the concepts of good and evil, virtue and vice, the warp and woof of consciousness and the mercurial nature of Man. More pillars. The glorious drive back from Kinsale with Ruth at his side, coming up over the Vee and down into the Sullane valley with the sun setting and their thoughts coalescing and between them a silent understanding that, having earlier experienced in the act of lovemaking the transmutation of lowly instincts into godly essence and accepting that moment as being so sublimely beautiful it could not be surpassed, death now was the only reply, the only fitting end to such ecstasy. Up ahead loomed a large overhead bridge under which stood a gigantic pillar of stone and, as they approached the bridge, he thought he heard a whispered *Yes* and that in that *Yes* she was willing him to turn the steering wheel a fraction of a revolution to the left and accelerate towards the pillar, thus transporting them to an exquisite bliss never before encountered. Such a desire to die in her company was, however, eclipsed by a greater desire to live in it.

What vivid, apocalyptic dream does he now recall?

The dream of Judgment Day that terrified him in the early hours of 5 February 2006, alone in the bedroom of the first-floor flat of 303 Harold's Cross Road, Dublin. In the dream he is standing at his bedroom window in Ardboe looking down on the lawn, which is a sea of white: men in white robes as far as the eye can see, men bowing down in prayer at the Hajj in Mecca. And there among them is his father, dressed from head to toe in white Muslim garb. A bell tolls and his mother and Lucy enter the room, pale and frightened. Suddenly it is clear: soon the trumpet will sound and the mountains will fold and the oceans will spill and the sky will split asunder. The hour is drawing near. Frantic with fear – he gives no thought to his mother or his sister nor they to him – he is running out of the city, heading west on the old Galway road. Beyond Kinnegad, Vinnie Molloy from the chicken factory approaches on a bike, then veers suddenly into a field and cycles in a wide arc to avoid Luke. Such a sinner is he, Luke, that Vinnie Molloy – the vilest of men – will not deign to pass him. When Luke woke up, the room was dark and the sky outside had a strange ominous hue. He lay in bed, petrified, certain it was the Last Day and there was no time left to right his wrongs, because Death will not wait. He ran to the window expecting to find the city in chaos and people hysterical. But the traffic crawled by as usual, car drivers staring calmly ahead. He turned on the radio. What was wrong with everyone, had they not heard? He dressed quickly, hands trembling, darting from window to door and back again, like a headless chicken. Frightened, heartsick, he left the house and walked down Harold's Cross Road, his legs like jelly. Hours later, standing in his classroom in Belvedere as the bell tolled for each new class, he finally accepted that the last ding-dong of doom had not yet sounded.

What action does he take on his arrival at the house?

He drops the plastic bag inside the front door, runs down the hall to the bathroom, evacuates his bowels in an urgent diarrhoeic splurge, then remains – in a weakened state – on the toilet bowl until he is confident that the last dregs are discharged from his bowels. Afterwards, bringing a higher than normal level of consciousness to bear on each task, he cleans himself, flushes the toilet and washes his hands. He exits the bathroom, collects the plastic bag, walks along the back hall to the kitchen and tumbles its contents onto the table.

What does he find?

Two bundles of personal correspondence comprising eighteen letters written by Ellen to Mossie Mulvey and nine photocopied letters written by Mulvey to Ellen, each neatly tied with string. A large brown envelope containing legal correspondence between Ellen's solicitors, Mahon and Keane, The Mall, Cork, and Mulvey's solicitors, Arnold & Whelan, South Parade, Waterford; a red document wallet containing legal documents that include a notice of motion, a statement of claim, orders for discovery, pleadings, affidavits, a notice for particulars, etc. In a separate envelope: a newspaper report and miscellaneous items of evidence including doctors' receipts, airfare receipts, character references, a medical report, and two photocopied letters labelled 'anonymous texts'.

After examination of the anonymous texts, does Luke concur with Ellen's belief that they were written by Mossie Mulvey?

As the texts appear to be written in a deliberately shaky hand and, considering the poor grammatical structure, misspellings, similarities of letter formation (e.g. the particular wobble on the upward stroke of the lower case *b* and the lower case *f*, the slant on the capital *T*) and how closely it resembles the handwriting in Mossie Mulvey's letters to Ellen should feeble attempts be made to disguise it, it is difficult not to conclude that those letters were written by Mulvey.

What specific claims and allegations were made in the anonymous letters?

The first letter stated that Ellen gave birth to a child in an unnamed New York hospital three years prior – which would have been 1960. The writer supplied the names of two people who could verify (and swear under oath, if necessary) this fact, and claimed that these people could show 'on a map of America' where exactly the child was being raised. The second letter urged Mossie Mulvey to stop making a fool of himself and to give up 'the old girl'. Ellen is later described as 'an old maid' who comes running home from America every summer, 'man-mad'. This letter claims that, prior to Mossie, two other 'decent men' from the town gave up Ellen after the letter writer intervened and 'put them right' about the kind of woman she was. The decent men are named but are unknown to Luke.

What new information is revealed in the personal letters?

That Mossie Mulvey was in no hurry to get married and would have been happy to stay single for the rest of his life but for the pressure he was under – from whom is not stated. That he accused Ellen of being 'forceful' and 'bossy'. That he consulted a mission priest who advised him not to marry until the woman's virtue was beyond question. That Ellen regularly sent him gifts – shirts, pants, razors. That Ellen was heartbreakingly earnest, entirely honest, often desperate and occasionally pushy. That Mossie Mulvey was wary, cagey, secretive and was, in all likelihood, whoring around the whole time he knew Ellen.

What random, incidental information is revealed in the letters?

That among the Clarks' possessions were a summer house on Martha's Vineyard, a villa in the Bahamas, a ranch in California, a plane, two yachts – one moored at Edgartown,

Massachusetts, the other in Nassau. That, though Mr Clark was a blue blood, the wealth originated with Mrs Clark – whose grandfather founded a pharmaceutical company. That Mr Clark was an alcoholic. That Mossie Mulvey was a poor speller. That Ellen watched the TV series *Men into Space*. That on St Patrick's night 1962 she attended a concert in Carnegie Hall featuring Joe Feeney and Carmel Quinn. That she was bereft when young Hubie Clark went away to school in Groton, Massachusetts. That the travel itinerary for Mr and Mrs Clark in the spring of 1962 included a cruise in the Caribbean and an overnight stay at the Dalton ranch in Texas before flying up to New York to attend a party at the Governor of Vermont's residence in Montpelier. That, at all times, Ellen worked behind the scenes, packing Clark bags, ironing Clark linen, rearing Clark children. That the first TV arrived in Ardboe in October 1963.

From the collection of documents and correspondence to hand, can Luke deduce how the legal case proceeded?

Yes. The accusation of defamation brought by the Plaintiff (Ellen) against the Defendant (Mulvey) consisted of 'making and spreading serious, unwarranted and wrong imputations against Ellen O'Brien's chastity and good name'. In his defence Mulvey denied falsely or maliciously publishing of the Plaintiff that she was unchaste, but admitted that he refused to marry her because of anonymous writings 'against her chastity' which he had received and which left him in 'insufferable doubt'. Ellen's senior counsel advised serving a notice of trial, but warned there was a risk of proceeding to trial and beating the lodgement of £780 that Mulvey had already made in the Court – a manoeuvre intended to defeat Ellen's claim. In a character reference, Mrs Clark praised Ellen's honesty and trustworthiness, stating she was 'part of this family' and 'one of God's people'. A medical report from Homer B. Goldin, M.D., a gynae-cologist and obstetrician of 2088 Park Avenue, New York, stated that Ellen's abdomen and breasts were free of striae, her pelvic floor was tight, her fundus was small and her hymen was intact, thus confirming that not only was she a virgin but she had never been delivered of a child. On Tuesday, 9 March 1965 the *Irish Times* published – between a notice of a point-to-point race meeting at Oldtown, Co. Meath and an article suggesting money may become obsolete – a court report entitled 'Breach Damages for Nurse' which described Ellen as an Irish nurse working in America and gave an account of the breach of promise and defamation case mentioned in the High Court the day before. The report revealed that the case had been settled on the terms that, as well as a public apology, Maurice Mulvey would pay Ellen O'Brien £1500 damages, £312 expenses and £480 costs.

After reading the files, what action does Luke take?

For an unknown and unmeasured number of minutes he remains seated at the table, physically arrested and emotion-ally disconcerted by the contents of the files and letters.

Amid the emotional disconcertment, what pleasing patch of reverie does he stray upon?

He recalls how, as a child, he had felt closely connected to the Clark family and had, for a time, believed they were related to his family and could therefore – and did, vicariously – partake of their glamorous lifestyle. The incidental details recorded in Ellen's letters now evoke a feeling of nostalgia associated with that time. *Tonight we had Mr Clark's law partners and their wives for dinner so I didn't get to bed until midnight . . . Mr and Mrs Clark are flying down to the Caribbean & boarding their boat for a month's cruise . . . Hubie had four college friends here for the weekend, they acted like a crowd of schoolboys and then they tell me they're men . . . I hope Mr Clark will straighten himself out and we can be a happy house again.*

Rising, finally, what does Luke do?

Rising and simultaneously pushing back his chair, he inclines his torso, spreads his arms and, with a sweeping motion, gathers the documents into a pile in the centre of the table. He then makes coffee, lights a cigarette, inhales, exhales, lifts his eyes to the clock on the wall and reads the time: five minutes past twelve.

What fear suddenly assails him?

The arrival of the noonday demon: the *evagatio mentis*, the weariness and loathing of life, the torpidity and lethargy that afflicts the minds, bodies and spiritual lives of its victims, alighting just as the sun reaches the highest point in the sky, bringing waves of sloth and sorrow, tedium, idleness and inertness, a soul sickness that caused, in medieval times, the most religious men and women to grow careless, listless and dejected until they raised their eyes in flight from work and gazed sleepily at walls, falling headlong into the paralysing sin of acedia.

Has he had prior visitations from the noonday demon?

Yes. It descends and enters him regularly and not only at noon and not always in its medieval form.

Enters him? In what form?

It announces itself with lethargy, torpidity, a wandering mind, thoughts that swing suddenly from the banal to the grandiose, the inflationary, the fantastical, and are frequently punctuated by a mental cataloguing of his own virtues, talents, aptitudes, abilities – all of which, he adduces, have gone entirely unnoticed and unappreciated by others for years (at least since the death of his mother). Remembrance of his virtues, talents and abilities provokes in him a remembrance of the dearth of virtues, talents and abilities in others and a remembrance of prior grudges and grievances directed at those employed in fields as far ranging as agriculture and the arts, and more specifically at those individuals who differ from him ideologically and whose mediocrity enrages him – precisely because they possess no ideological beliefs or stances. Said grievances ferment until they advance with incremental intensity from seething resentment to malevolence to an insatiable desire to see these mediocrities – who are now mortal enemies – vanquished, but not before he mentally enumerates their faults, failings and sins (ignorance, avarice, corruption, deception, cowardice, treachery, crime, cunning, cruelty, mendacity) while simultaneously listing and cursing the culprits – whose range, by the way, extends from the parochial (the town's supermarket proprietor, butcher, baker, property developer, two county councillors, two TDs) to the national (four government ministers, two ex-Taoisigh, the top brass of the Garda, the top brass at Hawkins House, the majority of priests, bishops and members of religious orders) to the global (the fathers of Western syphilisation and economic imperialism; the fathers of empire and bureaucratic cant; the pope, his cardinals and their yay-saying minions; the CEOs of giant corporations, big pharma, big oil, big capitalism; bigots, holocaust deniers, climate-change deniers, animal experimenters; Russia, China, the UK, the US, the state of Israel, the FBI, the CIA, MI5, Mossad, the 54 countries that supply extraordinary rendition, the multitudinous countries who supply ordinary rendition, the purveyors of FGM, circumcision and gay-bashing, the Charles Taylors, Baby Doc Duvaliers, Jean-Pierre Bembas and others), and whose number now include one Maurice Mulvey, deceased. In continuing frustration and agitation (but in tentative anticipation of a little antidotal *schadenfreude*), he begins to concoct fitting punishments to be meted out, where possible, by those who have suffered at the hands of the mediocrities. He occasionally idles hours away in such truncated, trancelike states, roused intermittently by a fresh surge of rancour. Then, mentally exhausted, he reaches a point of arrival that has nothing to offer and no path leading forward or back. It is at this point that, depending on the time of day and his fiscal situation, he either (a) surrenders to sleep or (b) opens another bottle of red wine and advances deeper into the *evagatio mentis*.

What mental attitude – followed by physical action – does he now adopt to fight the demon?

He suppresses the longing to curl foetally on the plum-coloured velvet sofa in the drawing room, resists even the temptation to cross his arms on the table, lay his head down and succumb to the seductive lure of sleep. Instead, after finishing his coffee and turning his body at an angle of approximately one hundred and twenty degrees to the left, he lifts one leaden foot and places it in front of the other and repeats the action until a fine stride is achieved and with such strides he leaves the kitchen, proceeds along the back hall, crosses the red-carpeted front hall and exits the house by the front door.

What bodily posture does Luke adopt on leaving the house?

He opens his mouth wide, lifts his face to the breeze blowing up from the river, feels the reassuring contact of his feet on the ground and the weight of flesh on his bones. He strides at a brisk pace, hands in pockets, head held high, down the avenue, the urge to light a cigarette thwarted by the realisation that his cigarettes are on the kitchen table. Cool fresh air flushes through his lungs. Then, a realisation, a trepidation: that the world is not as it had been this morning and that all that surrounds him – daylight, sky, green lawn, stone house, avenue, lone sycamore, old oaks and beeches, the distant rumble of a lorry, the pebbles resting at the grass verge, the cats prowling, the dog ambling from the yard, the sun about to glare on the glass of the front landing window as it does most days around noon – is not real. And that, if he permits this glancing thought (or realisation or trepidation) to take hold, his whole organism will intuit his fears and he will balk, like a child learning to cycle, and his feet will fail to ferry him and his body will not uphold him.

What dominant thoughts emerge from the riot of all others as he proceeds down the avenue?

That something not visible to him has set the events of the morning in motion. That he has entered a complex maze, a zone of danger. That he is completely alone now, *sans* father, *sans* mother, *sans* sister, *sans* aunt, *sans* lover. That he will forever sleep in his own arms.

What dominant memory emerges?

A morning when he was about three, observing his mother writing a letter at the kitchen table. Sunlight was streaming in the tall window. As she wrote a tear rolled down her face. Then she paused and shook her hand and blue ink fell onto the page and he thought the ink originated in her body and that it possessed some secret precious knowledge concerning his mother. The notion formed in him that any knowledge that is secret or precious or worth having passes through us in this fashion. A short time afterwards he learned to read and write and for some time after that he would sit at the kitchen table on the chair his mother had sat on and imagine the words in size and shape he supposed his mother had written that morning and strive to recreate them on his own page. He would look out and see the sycamore tree on the lawn and his father's Hereford cows in the field beyond the lawn, and though he did not look beyond the field at the line of trees on the river bank or at the stepped roofs of the town or the church steeple or the river itself, he was aware of them there in the periphery of his vision as they had been in the periphery of his mother's vision, and he had the sense that they – and the light coming in the window and the table and chairs and dresser and the air and atmosphere around her in the kitchen, and even his own presence – had flowed into his mother and mingled inside her and were constituent parts in the creation of her words. He cannot remember what, if anything, he produced, but when he sat there and strove to recreate her words, he felt, for a few moments, intense happiness, that he was in the glowing presence of his mother, a far warmer and more glowing presence than was ever afforded him in her actual presence. With only the vaguest sense of what he was after all his life, he now realises it is those mysterious words that came out of his mother's body onto the page and the ensuing feeling that the image of her that morning engendered that he has always hankered after, and he thinks this image of his mother in the window light has always existed in his mind as an enduring image of absence.

What feeling suddenly afflicts him?
    Dread.

*   *   *

What vision suddenly afflicts him?

His life rewound, run backwards. This existence now a subset of a larger hypothetical existence containing a house with an avenue and painted gates and a farm with tilled fields. A teeming house – an abode of bliss, a hypothetical marriage now unwound, hypothetical children running backwards/upwards/downwards on non-hypothetical stairs, going in and out of non-hypothetical rooms and cars and cots and beds, shrinking in size and retreating to toddlerhood, then infancy, then being packed back inside their hypothetical mother's womb, then said mother retreating down the avenue, back along the marriage years to the wedding, to her first appearance behind the windscreen of a little yellow car bouncing up the avenue. Other hypotheticals rewound, undone: the baby names Lara (originating in Larissa, daughter of Pelasgus, mortal princess of Argos, a moon orbiting Neptune) and Clara (from D.H. Lawrence), and Andrew and David (conveying refinement and culture); the dog's name Athos, loyal pet of Rudolph Bloom, Queens Hotel, Ennis; the family holidays, the people-carrier, the social life, the PT meetings, the teenage angst, the career choices – it is surely environmentalists, civil rights lawyers, MSF doctors he would engender. They would be tall. One might be gay . . . But, alas, all hope is gone now. This is the end of hope.

Why the end of hope?

Because there is no more Ruth.

* * *

Why no more Ruth? Did he not insist to Ellen that Ruth was innocent?

Innocent, yes, but the good is gone now. The damage is done. It was done fifty years ago and lay there waiting for them, like a snare. All that remains now is nostalgia for a lost future.

Is he certain?

He's certain of nothing.

What mental mathematical calculation does he now attempt?

He tries to calculate his exact age in days. With the primary operation (365×34) demanding more concentration than he is willing to muster up, he rounds the three-hundred-and-sixty-five upwards and the thirty-four downwards, and instantly arrives at a figure of twelve thousand. He knows Ellen for approximately twelve thousand days.

As opposed to?

Knowing Ruth for thirty days. During which they spent three overnights together (approximately 18 hours x 3), also parts of two Fridays (approximately 4 hours x 2), parts of three Saturdays (approximately 7 hours x 3), parts of four Sundays (approximately 6 hours x 4), which, in addition to talking on average 1.5 hours on the phone per night Mon–Thurs for four weeks, amounts to 131 hours, approximately, spent in each other's company.

* * *

At the end of the avenue what urgent action is he compelled to take?

He has to hunt Paddy back up the avenue. After waving his arms and shouting, the dog, alarmed, turns and trots back towards the house. Quickening his pace Luke passes between the piers and strides along the road towards the bridge.

What sound momentarily diverts his attention to the field on his right?

The sound of a horse pissing. A bay of approximately fourteen hands high stands inside the ditch, the tail held gracefully aloft as the hot stream falls heavily on the ground, hard after the dry summer to date. The rest of the horse – the head, the long pale face – remains motionless, in the manner of a sleeping horse. He thinks of the horses that served the farm before his time, then makes a mental list of the horse categories that have served man since time immemorial: farm horses, transport horses, war horses, ranch horses, race horses, wagon horses, circus horses, police horses, therapy horses, meat horses. He thinks of the horse latitudes, the equine graveyard somewhere in the calm, sub-tropical Pacific where, on long voyages to the colonies, horses were thrown overboard to lighten the load and save on water.

Looking to his right, what diverts his attention from the horse?

The glassy light of the river beyond the horse. The dark

woods beyond the river. The grey rooftops beyond the woods. The blue-grey sky beyond the rooftops.

What first alerted him to the presence of the river?

Bioacoustics. The sound world of living things, the song of trees and leaves, the syllables of rain. The vibrations he felt in the air on the riverbank one morning when he was ten, different from the vibrations on the lawn or in the yard or in the fields, different from those among humans or animals or buildings. Notes, softly rolling emanations, faintly whispering and falling from the branches and drifting over the water towards him, containing the measure and memory of trees and river, inseparable from each other for eons. Invisible spores, particles and vapours coalescing and swelling and rising in mist above the forest canopy and tumbling and rolling and frolicking in a joyousness invisible to all but him as he dissolved into the pulse of time and space and trees and river that morning.

Has he ever since experienced any similar dissolution of the self?

On certain late nights, alone, with the assistance of smooth jazz and approximately three glasses of red wine, a similar spiritual communion and exultation of the soul is experienced. On certain mornings, noons and nights, watching from the landing window as tricks of light and perspective conjure rainbows, fogbows, dawn spectres, white-outs, irradiated illusions brought on by snow, mist, cloud, distance, the blue hills of childhood, the imagined eyes of creatures looking out from the dark of woodlands. Transfixed, alert to every sound and movement, he is convinced in those moments that everything is connected and everything – every birdsong, every cloud scud, every movement of leaf or twig or branch – carries within it a cosmic message.

What urge, acute as he approaches the red iron bridge, forces him to turn back?

The urge to empty his bladder.

Turning in the avenue, what vision of the future suddenly confronts him?

The day when he'll be gone from here. The house and land and river will still exist. Ivy will snarl over the front door, over gutters and downpipes, creeping across window-panes. Slates will be missing, chimney pots collapsed. Musty old clothes in wardrobes, old sweet papers under beds. His Aussie niece or nephew or some hired hand will enter the rooms, dismantle beds and chandeliers, pack up the detritus of his life and of those that went before him and all the things he values and enjoys and are meaningful to him will be disposed of, and his time spent with them will be of no avail to him or to them. Objects will be wrenched from each other – cups separated from dressers, cutlery from drawers, pillows from mattresses, his boots parted from his knitted socks.

At what point does he urinate?

At approximately three-quarters of the way up the avenue,

under a beech tree, he stops, opens his fly and, letting out a low moan of relief, he urinates in a hot steady stream.

What urination practice does he now recall?

The male Muslim practice of sitting down while peeing as extolled to him by Rachid, the twenty-eight-year-old Libyan IT engineer he met in the Front Lounge bar one Saturday night in June 2007, and who, on three occasions, he kissed and fondled (and only kissed and fondled) in his (Rachid's) apartment in Monkstown, Rachid being a semi-celibate, fully conflicted gay man. Luke had assumed the sitting-while-pissing was practised out of consideration for women but learned that the practice is intended to safeguard men from urine soiling, the smallest trace of urine on the person or clothing of a Muslim being, according to the hadith of the prophet Muhammad, one of the greatest impediments to entering Heaven. No more hygienic a man than Rachid has Luke ever known.

Was Rachid circumcised?

Yes. Rachid's shyness and body modesty combined with (a) Luke's reluctance to cause embarrassment and (b) the mental image of the infant Rachid's genital mutilation prevented him from further enquiry or comment. In a light-hearted discussion on the topic weeks later he informed Rachid that the divine prepuce, aka the carnal bridal ring of the holy Catholic apostolic church, which was preserved in the village of Calcata near Rome for centuries, went missing in 1983.

*　*　*

Was Luke in love with Rachid?

Yes. From the moment, in Rachid's apartment, he caught a glimpse of him through a half-open door, praying. With his pure heart, simple truths and naïve beliefs he reminded Luke of no one more than Josie. I could convert to Islam, he offered, if it helps? He meant: if it helped Rachid to love him. Dear Luke, he replied, in your heart you are already Muslim, insha'Allah. Anyway, he said, you would be *reverting*, not *converting* — reverting to the original state to which your soul was destined. Luke was a little in love with Islam too. For some time after he ceased seeing Rachid he continued the practice of sitting while urinating.

What aspects of Islam was he in love with?

The practice of Zakat, the obligation to give ten per cent of one's wealth to the poor. The practice of eating only with the right hand, and using the left only to clean oneself in the toilet (this too he practised until he didn't). The belief that there are a hundred names for God; that if you loan to Allah a beautiful loan He will return it tenfold; that the reason birds sing is to praise Allah. The story concerning Muhammad's kindness to animals as relayed by Leopold Bloom when he sees a tabby on a windowsill on Cumberland Street: the prophet, on finding a cat asleep on his mantle, cut a piece off the garment so as not to disturb the sleeping cat. The story concerning Muhammad's kindness to his fellow man as relayed to Luke by Rachid: every day, for years, Muhammad's neighbours dumped their rubbish outside his door, and every day Muhammad disposed of it without complaint. Then one day, finding no rubbish outside his door, Muhammad ran, worried, to the neighbours' door, thinking they must be ill. Rachid told a story about himself, too: whenever he received sweets from his father as a small boy, he ate half of them and put the other half aside for Allah.

To what are Luke's eyes drawn as he zips up?

To the cracks and fissures on the east-facing wall of the house. To the sprigs of wild rocket sprouting at intervals from these new cracks and fissures.

What causes him to frown?

Concern that the appearance of these new cracks is evidence that the foundation of the house has been compromised as a result of his own actions six summers ago.

What happened six summers ago?

Josie died. In the days following her funeral Luke investigated the enigma of the partly concealed Georgian windows at the lower-ground level of the house. With no other evidence of the existence of a basement – no door or stairway or other customary means of access to a basement – these windows had always baffled him. His hunch was that during construction of the house in the 1830s, the basement area was never fully dug out and cleared of earth, but was left as it was, incomplete.

Was there a concealed basement?

Yes. The day after Josie's funeral he descended the stone

steps that led from the back door down to garden level and with a pick-axe and sledgehammer he broke open a hole in the wall under one of the mysterious windows, then gouged at the wall around the window, loosened the frame and, as night fell, removed the sash window in two sections. Inside, he found a high bank of earth. On the second day he dug like a madman. With shovel, spade and wheelbarrow, blood, sweat and tears, and Josie always on his mind, he carved a path into the bank of earth and dug through the dark centre of the house until he could go no further. On the third day he hired a mini-digger and a driver and two local lads from the town and they brought out earth and dislodged stones that were packed hard to almost ceiling height, and for the first time in one hundred and seventy years, daylight, fresh air and human activity entered those dark musty chambers. Every day they dug and filled wheelbarrows and brought out earth and, slowly, three large cave-like rooms with flag-stone floors and load-bearing walls revealed themselves. In the evenings, dirty, sweaty and with aching bones, Luke and the men sat out on the front lawn drinking beer and eating supermarket pizza dickied up with extra cheese and onions by his mother and served on a wooden chopping board. On Saturdays and Sundays he toiled alone, stripped to the waist, maniacal in his grief. At night, his mind raced with plans and high hopes for this newly discovered space – the hosting of weddings, literary festivals, yoga weekends, retreats. Occasionally, niggling worries that he had not engaged an engineer to verify the safety of the structure surfaced. One night, when the work was complete and the space cleaned,

166

he brought down a kitchen chair and a power cable and strung up lights and sat in the underground cave watching his shadow dance on the walls.

What image is suddenly called to mind now?

The image of his child-aunt Una in a white dress and veil on the occasion of her First Holy Communion in 1938, the photograph of which he found in an envelope in the furthest corner of the dark, angled, low-ceiling space under the stairs on the morning he commenced work on the basement. Unsmiling, with full lips and an intense determined gaze (of what? – holiness or defiance or knowledge?), her pale wide face still haunts him.

What other remnants of this child-aunt did he find under the stairs on that morning six years ago?

Her school satchel, which, after seventy years in the dark, he brought out into the hall light. Fashioned from recycled leather, as evidenced by the awl-bored holes of previous stitching, it had a rudimentary metal buckle and a crude leather tab sewn on with crooked stitches. Old mould stains had accumulated on the stiff unforgiving leather. He had an image of her father, perhaps, late at night under candlelight, working on the satchel, or the local cobbler, surgeon to old shoes and satchels, pushing a needle through the tough leather, pricking and prodding his fingertips, going to the bone. There, waiting for her on the kitchen table the next morning, all hers. When he opened the rusting buckle that day, minute ferrous flakes fell on the carpet. A silence of pity fell on him. He lifted out the contents – books, copybooks, a pink pencil stump, the point roughly pared with a knife or blade. He read the titles. *Léightheoirí Proinnias Naomhtha, An Dreoilín; Drámaí Scol, Íosogán, Pádraig Mac Piarrais; Plain Song for Schools, Part Two; Grammar; Stair na hÉireann; Tír-eolas na hÉireann; Brown & Nolan's No. B School Jotter; The 'Eclipse' Exercise Book* with the name 'Una O'Brien' and a date, 24.10.40, on the perforated line at the bottom. A scrapbook covered in embossed wallpaper contained pieces of fabric, sewing samples displaying the hemming stitch, top-stitch, button-holes, each sample labelled and dated from 13 June 1940 to 11 December 1940.

Why were his hands shaking?

At the realisation that hers – his child-aunt's – were probably the last hands that touched those pages. That she had probably arrived home from school on the day of the Christmas holidays in December 1940, and flung the satchel under the stairs, not needing it again until a few weeks later. Molecules of her sweat, her touch DNA, still detectable on the strap.

Did he read the contents of the jotter or copybooks that morning?

He leafed through a mix of essays, sums, grammar exercises and a night-time prayer in the jotter. Neatly written joined handwriting, the capital letters extending to the top line, the ticks and corrections marked up in a teacher's red pen, now faded to pink. Essay titles, in chronological order:

The Wood in Winter, St Rita, Sun Down, Lourdes and Bernadette, History of the Danes, Oíche Shamhna, Rubber, Eight Sentences on Diarmuid. In the copybook, a mix of English, Irish and geography exercises: Meaning of the poem 'Adare'; Counties of Ireland, Lessons We Learned, Ports of Ireland, Pattern Day; an Irish grammar exercise on the Tuiseal Ginideach; a letter to a friend dated 5 December 1940; a second essay on Winter.

What impression of his child-aunt did he form from her writings?

That she was a child of earnestness, innocence, sincerity, obedience, compliance, adherence to religious practice; one who possessed an average intelligence and a certain formality; a neat handwriter.

What were the final entries?

19 December: *Winter is the saddest season of the year because its birds are gone to distant countries at the most time we want them. The woods in Clonduff look very dreary because their beautiful clothes are withered and they are cold and bear and always shivering.*

20 December: *Mary Mother, fold me tight, In your arms throughout the night. Guide me on my shadowed way; Shield me till the dawn of day. Guide me till the dark is past. Bring me to God's home at last. Amen.*

What penny suddenly drops now?

The startling coincidence that his child-aunt Una and his beloved James Joyce both departed this world in January

1941, Una at approximately 11 a.m. GMT (assuming death occurred on impact) on the first day of the month, James at 2.15 a.m. CET on the thirteenth day of the month; Una in west Waterford, James in the Schwesternhaus vom Roten Kreuz in Zurich; their departures separated by eleven days, fifteen hours and fifteen minutes and by a distance of 1289 kilometres over land and sea. The further realisation — accompanied by a racing heart — that at the approximate time his child-aunt was penning those final exercises in her jotter Joyce had recently arrived in Zurich and installed his little family in the Hôtel Pension Delphin, sick and broken and preoccupied with Lucia, spending the days before Christmas wandering in the snow along the Zurichsee or watching the water at the confluence of the Sihl and Limmat rivers. Both man and child oblivious to the disaster that was floating close. Luke is confounded that, despite the innumerable occasions that the words 'January 1941' crossed his mind and tongue throughout his life, he had, until this very moment, failed to notice this coincidence.

What images flow from this coincidence?

Two souls alighting from two recently rendered unconscious temporal abodes, one situated at the bottom of a brick-walled well, the other on a bed in a dimly lit hospital ward, one prone, the other supine. Each soul then ascending the stratospheres, moving through dark space, in and out among the cold stars, passing each other at intervals until Joyce's soul, moved by curiosity and a vague memory of other small souls, reaches out to the little girl and, hand in hand, they roam the heavens, in among the Moons of Jupiter, over the Rings of Saturn and when they orbit planet Earth he points at the dot that is Dublin and tells her of its beauty and eccentricities and he dances a little jig and sings a little ditty and she laughs till she cries at his quirks and his quarks and his puns.

What other images flow from this coincidence?

The grave at Fluntern. The white skin. The darkness within. The military blood. The spirochete still at last.

Who calls Luke's name as he approaches the front door?

Brian Lynch, stepping up into the cab of the John Deere in the adjoining field, his hand in descent following a salute.

How does Luke respond?

He moves his head and body ninety degrees to the left and raises his hand in a reciprocal gesture, the glimpse of Brian Lynch reminding him of his attractiveness and causing him to surmise that if he, Luke, were a woman, he would surely give thought to the handsome babies Brian would sire, and with this thought he then recalls the occasion, years ago, when Brian and his father brought a maiden heifer over to their yard to be serviced by their bull, aka the Master, and the two young boys stood watching as the Master was led into the pen and sniffed around the heifer for several minutes until finally he mounted her, at which point Luke's father reached in and with his bare hand guided the Master's pizzle into the heifer. *Baculum baculorum!*

Stepping into the hall, what does he do?
He dials Ruth Mulvey's number.

Does she reply?
No, the call goes to her mailbox. He listens to her voice, then hangs up, his heart pounding, his hand trembling, a thousand thoughts and feelings swarming his mind.

What kind of thoughts and feelings?
Confused, conflicting, oscillating thoughts. He wants to see her. He does not want to see her. He wants to talk to her. He does not want to talk to her. He wants to tell her everything. He wants to tell her nothing. He loves her. He doesn't know her. He knows her thirty days. He knows her one hundred and thirty-one hours.

What does he do?
He puts the phone in his pocket, sits on the green velvet chaise longue, removes his shoes, reclines his back and stares at the framed picture on the opposite wall above the fireplace, judging – not for the first time – the frame too narrow for the picture.

What does the picture depict?
In a dark, gloomy, navy-blue watery underworld a

frogman is suspended in a diagonally descending diving position.

What is the picture's provenance?

Luke bought the etching, entitled *Diving for Pearls*, at a charity art exhibition in the hospice in Harold's Cross on his way home from work on 5 December 2004. Cost, remembered: €170. Artist's name forgotten, but handwritten on a label stuck to the back of the picture.

What other watery image now comes to mind?

The Dream of the Fisherman's Wife that he once came upon in a book on (mostly lesbian) Shunga in Watkins Books on Cecil Court in London. The image was of a woman in a sexual pose with two octopuses, a daddy octopus and a son octopus, the daddy performing cunnilingus on the woman and the son fondling her mouth and nipple. Tentacles all over her body, the mollusc sucker's mouth buried in her furry vulva, the woman apparently in raptures. Intelligent creatures, octopuses, they can think for themselves. Tentacle touch must be delicious for a woman. All touch is delicious.

Following contemplation of the picture, what does Luke do?

He rises, walks along the back hall into the kitchen, begins to pack the letters and files into the plastic bag. He pauses mid-task, glances across the room at the empty fireplace, then completes the task and leaves the bag of files on the floor, propped against the wall. He empties the coffee pot, refills it and puts it on the hob to brew.

What significance attaches to the coffee pot?

It is a Bialetti Rainbow 3-cup in light blue (with an accumulation of coffee stains running vertically from the lid downwards), a gift from Ruth Mulvey after the glass beaker of his previous cafetiere broke, purchased on Thursday, 28 June in TK Maxx, Cornmarket Street, Cork.

While the coffee brews, what thoughts on the subject of chance occur to him?

In a town with a population of 759, of unknown male/female ratio, what were the chances that he and she would meet and, worse, be unknown to each other up to then and, worse still, fall in love? *What were the chances?* But the thing about chance that he has always known – chance or risk or probability – is *its absolute truth*. Truth is told clearly in probability and the beauty of that truth is that it is logical. Why, given all the possibilities, only one outcome *actually* happens? But a thing only needs to happen once to prove probability. In the very long run, *everything* happens, everything is inevitable. Why are we surprised by this?

After pouring his coffee, what does he do?

He lifts the plastic bag containing the files onto the table, selects four items (the notice of motion, one anonymous letter, the gynaecologist's report and the newspaper clipping) and photographs them with his phone camera. He brings his phone to his study down the hall, uploads the photographs to his laptop, opens his Gmail and composes an email to Ruth Mulvey:

Dear Ruth,

I tried to call you earlier. I discovered today that your father was once engaged to Ellen. He broke off the engagement and humiliated her by making false accusations against her and spreading lies. He said he had received anonymous letters claiming she had a child in America. She had no option but to take him to court to clear her name.

I didn't believe Ellen at first. It seemed too far-fetched. But she showed me the legal files – the letters, the court documents, the newspaper reports from March 1965. Ellen O'Brien, Ardboe House, Clonduff is the Plaintiff, and your father, Maurice Mulvey, Curraboy, Clonduff is the named Defendant. I have them here. I'll photograph and attach some for you. There's no doubting the truth of all this.

Needless to say, I knew nothing, and I'm assuming you didn't either and this will floor you as much as it has me.

Ellen is very distressed. My heart is breaking thinking of all she has suffered. Her whole life was blighted as a result of what happened. There are probably still people around who believe the lies he told about her.

She wants me to stop seeing you. Please do not

think I am doing this lightly. This is an awful mess.
My heart is doubly breaking. But I have to think
about Ellen. She's old and she has only me. I'm sorry.
I cannot abandon her. I hope you understand.
  Luke x

What doubt must Luke now admit to himself?

A doubt that has assailed him almost every day in recent weeks: that, despite her best intentions and earnest efforts, Ruth has had great difficulty understanding and accepting his sexuality, and this problem would, he fears, eventually come between them.

What else?

That, even if he wanted to continue with Ruth, and even if Ellen gave the relationship her blessing, this revelation of her father's mistreatment of Ellen would always cast a shadow on the union; it would always be the elephant in the room.

Does Ellen's threat to disinherit him have a bearing on his decision?

It does not. If, in his core, he believed that remaining with Ruth was the right thing to do, nothing would dissuade him otherwise — certainly not the promise of money or property. He is doing what his conscience can tolerate. The prospect of inflicting further pain on his aunt is unconscionable.

Does he send the email?

He checks it for mistakes, attaches the four photographs,

hits 'Send', logs out of his Gmail account, closes his laptop and returns to the kitchen and his coffee.

What image of Ruth Mulvey crosses his mind?

The night she knelt on his bed and held his head in her hands like a globe, like Eliot's doctor, and announced she would unkink the brain waves and cure his sadness. Listen, listen, she pleaded, you see yourself as a victim, a tragic victim, *glittering* even . . . He clung to her, crying, and then made love to her and went far inside her and she begged him to go deeper and, no longer afraid of injuring her, he went deep in mind and body, among crowded organ cavities, past the contours of her lungs and liver, and, shimmying past her heart, he felt her perfection. The next morning at dawn they walked on the riverbank in silence. Moving under low branches in the peace of the river, they were joined in perfect captivity. No needs or wants or musts, the feeling that within those moments, in the drift of that silence, was held all of eternity. Afterwards when the other world returned and birds came out and he was stirred out of the trance, vapour rose from the surface of the water and small waves lolled at his feet and without ever saying a word they knew they had been party to something that neither could name.

Other images of her?

Awake at night tormented by the suffering of laboratory animals. Walking into the inner yard of a flats complex in the north inner city, past boarded-up windows with graffiti, climbing a stairwell strewn with litter and used syringes and stinking of urine. Standing, at dawn, at a window high up in the penthouse suite of the Coombe Hospital looking out over the city's rooftops to the Dublin mountains with the sun rising into a clear blue sky, thinking of her husband driving home through the quiet streets, stopping at the lights, entering their empty house, as the little corpse she gave birth to the night before lay in a fridge somewhere in the hospital. At her desk now, this minute, a slight worry starting to form, a vague intuition that something is wrong.

Telepathically aware of her then?

Any telepathic connection, if one ever existed, is now severed.

Has he ever experienced telepathic connection with another human being?

All his life until her death he and Josie picked up the tiny vibrations of each other's mind. A streaming across, mutual phase locking, beautiful economic laziness, entrainment. The synchronisation of an organism (Josie to Luke) to an external rhythm (Luke to Josie). Biomusicology. Chronobiology. He knows that if you mount two clock pendulums side by side on a wall, they'll pick up the tiny vibrations of each other transmitted through the wall and their swings will gradually synchronize because matter is lazy and it takes less energy to pulse in synch than in opposition. He and Josie pulsed in synch, oscillated inside each other's psychic sphere, vibrated rhythmically until their neural pathways and circadian systems aligned and their cellular, sub-cellular, molecular, atomic and sub-atomic frequencies were synchronised. If he had been a woman he's certain their menstrual cycles would have aligned.

What is his theory about Josie's disability?

That on 1 January 1941, at the age of two years and three months, having in all likelihood witnessed the fall of her older sister down the well, she suffered a catastrophic rupture to her tender psyche which rendered her mute for the following two years until one day, when her mother ordered her to take off her wet clothes and dry them by the fire, an emphatic *No* sprang from her tongue. The rupture, exacerbated by the sudden departure of her father six months later on 16 June 1941, is proof positive to Luke how malleable human nature is during those sensitive moments that ethnologists call 'points of imprint vulnerability' and may have occasioned the acquisition of, or reversion to, primitive senses or pre-natal faculties (akin to those of animals) that compensated for the damage to the normal faculties and enabled her, Josie, to commune with birds.

Has the psychic connection to Josie extended beyond the grave?

Alive, she had been his mainstay. Now he imagines her delicate spirit adrift around him, beyond his view, in an alternative parallel universe suffused with subtle bodies. At unguarded moments he longs for her proximity, tries to tune into her frequency or into whatever of her has endured beyond physical death.

He believes in an afterlife then?

Though he has a liking for Catholic doxology and is fond of Stephen Dedalus's assertion that God is a shout in the street and the cheer of a goal scored, he is averse to the teachings and doctrines of all organised religions. However, there was never a time when he was not conscious of eternity, of something on-going – not so much a corporeal as a *psychic* continuation in some afterlife or aftermath of this existence. He thinks some archetypal image of eternity is present in him – in all souls – and has been from the beginning of time and that at death he will shrug off this physical form but leave something behind: his entelechia.

What, at the moment of death, does he think happens?

He was only ever present at one passing: Josie's. She expired quietly, each breath growing slower and shallower than the previous until they petered out and she was gone, this memory of her gentle death a comfort always, especially in light of the teachings of Islam – the credo which declaims the boldest dogma and offers the most graphic description of dying (and which, having been described in great awe and detail by Rachid, is the easiest to recall). In Islam the angel of death arrives and draws the soul out of the mouth, dragging it up through the body from the soles of the feet. Depending on the life lived and the deeds done by that individual, the evacuation of the soul will either be smooth and painless or a terrible sight to behold (gagging, retching, heaving, choking). Luke suspects the hour of our death is foreknown, inscribed on our timeline and waiting for us in everything connected to us — like a death notice or a pre-prepared obit embedded in every moment and object of our lives: in our tears, in the clothes we wear, in the rooms we sleep in, on the food set before us, in the ovaries, even, of our foremothers. And everything, with the exception of our own rational minds, implicitly 'knows' this. But by some merciful mechanism, the hour of our extinction — or exten-sion — is unknown to us.

Does Luke believe in the Islamic theory of passing?

It is not a theory but a belief, one he finds imaginatively and figuratively compelling but regrets that (a) it is attached to a plethora of primitive religious beliefs and practices which — like all religions — have more social, cultural and historical bases than spiritual ones and (b) it is interpreted by earnest devout Muslims in a literal rather than in a symbolic sense, thus causing great anticipatory fear and unnecessary distress around death beds.

What suddenly falls across his mind?

Darkness suddenly falls across his mind.

Caused by?

An image of his aunt as he left her this morning. The image of her sitting in the room all day, slowly passing each hour. The thought of all the hours and all the days and all the years that he was unaware of her suffering.

What other images followed by what word cross his mind?

A New York street on a May morning, a woman clutching a piece of paper on which is scribbled an address, a Park Avenue doorman directing her to the elevator and the fifth-floor suite of rooms. A tall, grey-haired patrician in a white coat. Her hush-dark fallopian tubes, her tender-pink womb in eternal waiting. The word *intact*.

What are his thoughts or feelings on Maurice Mulvey?

He tries, but is unable to form a picture of the physical man. A dark shadowy figure, like a character in a noir film, flits in and out of his consciousness, sometimes with Ellen close by. Then, remembering her suffering, he is usurped by a flood of rage. It is, he thinks, the epitome of evil to do what Mulvey did. He is baffled at how any man could do such a thing – what could drive a man to behave like that? Pure innate evil? Or the imp of the perverse? No, pure evil.

Why, suddenly, is Luke reminded of Raskolnikov?

Because he is a sinner, and it was the sinner, the psychology of sinners and the spread of darkness in the human soul that interested Dostoevsky. That interests Luke too, nothing human being alien.

*   *   *

Does this mean Luke is attempting to understand or even forgive Maurice Mulvey — wasn't Raskolnikov driven by the imp?

There is no comparison. Raskolnikov committed murder. But Raskolnikov was driven by hunger and poverty and his guilt sent him into a tormented state, and eventually he confessed his crime. Mulvey was never in such dire circumstances, nor did he ever confess his crime. If he had doubts or misgivings about the impending marriage he could simply have called it off and walked away. And, judging by the short time it took him to find a replacement bride, he wasn't too troubled or guilt-ridden. No agenbite of inwit. As for the imp . . . This is the only mitigating circumstance Luke might allow: that Mulvey's behaviour might have been the result of a deterioration of the cognitive control network in the lateral prefrontal cortex — the imp resides in the orbitofrontal cortex. But Luke doubts this was the case — there appears to be no evidence, either before or after his crime, of the usual display of disinhibited behaviours typically associated with the imp. As for forgiveness, it is not for Luke to forgive.

What disturbing thought regarding Ruth Mulvey now surfaces?

The sins of the father. The stain in the biology, in the blood. She herself may be entirely good and pure of heart — he thinks she is. But what of her inheritance? What if a genetic predisposition for cruelty exists in mankind — some as yet unidentified genetic variant in a particular enzyme, that, combined with certain environmental factors, could trigger the cruelty? She might be a carrier. It might skip a generation, like red hair and twins, or it might remain latent for ever. But he would always be afraid. In the furthest, darkest corner of his mind he would be waiting for the streak of cruelty to rear its head – if not in her, then in their offspring. He might be a carrier himself, the flawed pedigree inherited from the grandfather of unknown provenance who came over the mountains from Tipperary, a man who might have been as great – or greater – a liar and deceiver as Mossie Mulvey. What then? Her cruel gene *in connunctio* with his cruel gene. He might engender liars and thieves and frauds. He might bear a daughter who, one day, would turn on him and accuse him of the most heinous crimes against her.

What pleasures does he anticipate for the evening ahead?

The preparation of the evening meal, the drawing out of a cork from the neck of a bottle, the light fading, the cat at his feet, the evening his own as he cooks, eats, drinks and reads in the all-consuming, immersive manner of his youth.

Prompted by these thoughts, what does he do?

He extinguishes his cigarette in the ashtray, crosses the kitchen to the fridge, audits its contents: the remains of a 254g block of Kerrygold butter in its ragged wrapper; a block of Dubliner white cheddar, unopened; three lamb chops in a white plastic bag; three Portobello mushrooms; two cooked potatoes; a large tub of out-of-date Greek yogurt; five slices of granary bread; half a loaf of

McCambridge's wholemeal bread; in the salad box: a half bag of withered rocket leaves, three carrots, seven Piccolo tomatoes, half a cucumber, three wilted scallions, one red pepper, scraps of blackened leaves and sprigs, several spots of mould; on the door shelves: one unopened litre of milk, three eggs, a half-empty jar of Bonne Maman strawberry jam, an assortment of plastic bottles and glass jars containing salad dressings, ketchup, mayonnaise, mustard; a bottle of Coca-Cola, three-quarters full. He closes the fridge, opens the lower-right press of the waxed pine dresser, audits the alcohol: a bottle of Tempranillo, a bottle of Merlot, a half bottle of Jameson whiskey, a small bottle of Southern Comfort, two-thirds full.

What, in his opinion, are the merits of red wine over spirits?

A gentler sensory experience on the palate, a more fitting and sublime accompaniment to food, a wider and more varied availability of product, a more affordable cost, the aesthetic superiority of the receptacle – stemmed glass versus tumbler; a preference, on his part, for the refracted glow of purple over the refracted glow of amber through glass, the olfactory delights of aromatic oak, berry, cinnamon; the interesting and imminently more readable bottle labels; the voluminous quantity that can be consumed relative to its intoxicating effects thereby increasing the pleasure ratio; the gentler and more gradual slide towards intoxication, the lower alcoholic strength accounting for a lower gradation of hangover and thenceforth a lower level and intensity of hallucinatory and paranoiac thoughts in the days following a binge.

The assessment of spirits can be summed up as a *via negativa* of the above.

What occupies Luke during the late afternoon and early evening hours?

At 3.05 p.m., carrying a mug of sweet milky tea and two slices of toasted McCambridge's wholemeal bread topped with Dubliner cheddar, a sliced tomato and a pinch of salt, he re-enters the study, and, with no particular task or strategy in mind and with minimum awareness of the passage of time, a total of two hours and forty-four minutes pass before he exits the room again.

Describe the study.

Thirteen by twenty-one feet long, height unknown, but adhering to the Golden Ratio; walls painted in Farrow & Ball's Dix Blue, an area of damp visible on the top left corner under the cornice; directly opposite the door one twelve-paned Georgian window faces east; under the window a white double radiator; a Persian rug, predominantly red in colour but now faded and threadbare in patches, covers two-thirds of the floor, the remaining sixteen-inch-wide exposed border at the edge is painted in black; from the ceiling rose hangs a twelve-candle Waterford Crystal chandelier with eight candle bulbs inserted, purchased along with four other chandeliers as 'seconds' from the liquidation sale at the Waterford Crystal factory following the closure of the plant in May 2005 (the imperfections caused by the entrapment of air bubbles during the blowing process are barely visible); on the right wall, centred: a black cast-iron fireplace surrounded by hand-painted tiles depicting the god Apollo driving a herd of cows backwards; covering almost the entire left wall: four tightly stocked floor-to-ceiling oak bookshelves bought from a salvage yard in Cork city; positioned directly in front of the window: a large oak office desk with a small brass plate stamped with the manufacturer's name, location and date attached to the desk's underside, purchased at the liquidation sale of the Waterford Crystal factory; to the left of the desk a grey, metal, four-drawer filing cabinet with a small key inserted in the lock of the topmost drawer; to the right of the desk two further wooden bookshelves, set into the alcove to the left of the fireplace. On the desk a black Toshiba laptop, a brown glass ashtray full to the brim with cigarette butts and ash, a black mug emblazoned with two Joshua trees and the words 'Mazatlan, Mexico' – a gift from a Belvedere pupil and now a receptacle for pens, pencils, coloured markers, a scissor, ruler and elastic bands; a spiral-bound notebook on whose first page is handwritten a To Do list (bank, accounts balancing, vet, ideas of making money); at the centre of the desk, propped open on a wooden bookstand: a Penguin edition (1992) of *Ulysses* with an introduction by Declan Kiberd and the cover showing a photograph of the Martello Tower at Sandycove overlaid with two excerpts – the novel's opening lines presenting stately, plump Buck Mulligan and the closing from Molly Bloom's soliloquy and in the air surrounding it the ineluctable modality of the invisible.

*   *   *

What memories, feelings and sensations are elicited as he crosses the room?

From the rug underfoot: a memory from childhood of entering this room after his Saturday evening bath wearing only his underpants, then lying belly-down on the rug and reading *The Red Balloon*. From the sight of the filing cabinet: the occasion of the reading of his father's will (a copy of which now lies, along with a copy of Ellen's will, in the second drawer of the filing cabinet) the day after his burial, in the presence of his mother, Lucy, Josie, Ellen and the family solicitor Anthony J. Flynn. From the wall of books: a mild, gentle breeze of recognition, an easeful presence, the comfort of knowing that the characters who once provided rare fellowship and evoked in him deep sorrow, soaring raptures and some of the sublimest moments of his life to date, are still there where he left them and, for an instant, he still finds it hard to conceive that these characters are without individual agency.

List the contents of the metal filing cabinet.

In the two uppermost drawers: suspension files holding bank statements, utility bills, receipts, miscellaneous legal documents, tax returns, land leasing contracts with Jim Lynch stretching back over fourteen years, copies of forestry contracts, correspondence and grant applications relating to Coillte and Coillte information booklets on forestry. In the third drawer: further miscellaneous legal documents and solicitors' letters pertaining to his father's will, the sale of the milk quota in 2001, two bank loans; the deeds of the house, various family members' birth and death certs, two pages, stapled, downloaded from *Griffith's Valuation 1868, Boundary and Land Valuation of Ireland*; a black velvet case containing his father's gold pocket-watch; four stapled pages of an article entitled 'The Biological Evidence of River Capture' downloaded from JSTOR and originally published in the *Bulletin of the American Geographical Society* Vol. 37, No. 3 (1905). In the fourth and bottom drawer: a large lever-arch file subdivided with orange, green and blue card dividers titled Fiction, Poetry, Drama, each section containing hand-written lecture notes from his English degree courses at University College Dublin; three orange card folders containing lesson plans devised during his first year of teaching at Belvedere College: miscellaneous notes on miscellaneous writers and poets including Shakespeare, Austen, Joyce, Kavanagh, Plath, Bishop.

Of what relevance are the photocopied pages from *Griffith's Valuation*?

They contain the records of the previous proprietors of Ardboe House and lands which the O'Brien family has now occupied for three generations.

What do the records show?

At the time of valuation in the 1860s a Mr Matthew Wheeler was leasing this property from Sir Philip Chearnley of the nearby Saltertown House when it was valued at £28. Previously the site of Ardboe Castle (the ruins of which lie in the south-western corner of Luke's land), this land formerly belonged to the Knights Templar, who had an outpost a few miles downriver at Templemichael and were stationed at Rhincrew. There is no mention of Luke's grandfather and namesake, Luke O'Brien, who bought – or, at any rate, came into possession of – the land and house in 1928, having relocated from the larger property and lands a mile downriver at Coole Quay (a wedding gift from his in-laws), the site of the original old ford where St Fachtna crossed the river on his pilgrimage to Doonbeg.

Does he eat his bread and drink his tea?

Before sitting at the desk he makes room for the plate and the mug by sliding the laptop to the right and moving the bookstand to the top left corner. He sits and eats the laden bread, oblivious to the crumbs and the corner of brittle crust that drop to the plate. He drinks the tea until there remains approximately three teaspoons in the bottom of the mug, a habit he inherited from his father who believed that dust, dirt, sand, sediment and particles of other unknown matter sank and accumulated at the bottom of liquid receptacles such as buckets, milk jugs, tea cups, drinking glasses, etc., an opinion with which Luke the son concurs. The son consubstantial with the father.

List the books as they are arranged, left to right, on the two shelves immediately to the right of his desk.

The Mystery of Physical Life by E.L. Grant Watson.

The Hidden Reality by Brian Greene.

The Running Sky by Tim Dee.

The Illustrated Guide to the Sullane and Ardglass by Rev. Samuel Hyman.

Ulysses on the Liffey by Richard Ellmann.

The Classical Greek Reader edited by Kenneth J. Atchity.

H_2O and the Waters of Forgetfulness by Ivan Illich.

The Sea Around Us by Rachel Carson.

Complete Poems by Elizabeth Bishop.

James Joyce & the Burden of Disease by Kathleen Ferris.

A Reader's Guide to Finnegans Wake by William York Tindall.

The History of Sexuality by Michel Foucault (Vols 1, 2 and 3).

The Character of Consciousness by David J. Chalmers.

Collected Poems by Hart Crane.

The Lord Chandos Letter by Hugo Von Hofmannsthal.

Housekeeping by Marilynne Robinson.

Invisible Cities by Italo Calvino.

Atomised by Michel Houellebecq.

Wild by Jay Griffiths.

Elizabeth Costello by J.M. Coetzee.

Which books, or portions therein, left a lasting impression?

The sex scenes in *Atomised*. The soap ingredients listed on the soap-wrapper in *Elizabeth Costello*: 'Treblinka – 100% human stearate'. The say, say, say scene in *Housekeeping* where the long-submerged train leaps back up out of Lake Fingerbone and the resurrected passengers disembark at the station and walk home, calm and serene, to their lunch. The bell-rope that gathers God at dawn in 'The Broken Tower'. The trapped rats in their death throes gnashing their teeth and staring into the abyss in *The Lord Chandos Letter*. The discovery in *The Illustrated Guide to the Sullane and Ardglass* that the cherry was first domesticated less than a mile away in Norristown Castle. That said castle was home to the aristocratic healer of scrofula, Valentine Greatrakes, born on 14 February 1628, grandson of Sir Edward Harris, the 2nd Justice of the King's Bench in Ireland. That said scrofula healer (and now he recalls that a slut in Nighttown combs the tats from the hair of a scrofulous child) spent a year in contemplation in Ardboe Castle, and was a lieutenant in Cromwell's army before giving everything up – not unlike the Buddha – to roam the countryside laying hands on the sick and curing the afflicted. That the pile of stones comprising the remains of Norristown Castle (why Hyman described them as 'a curious ruin' is a mystery to Luke) lies in a field equidistant from the south-eastern boundary of Luke's land and Coole Quay. And tucked in among the details of the landed gentry and their family marriages, the coincidental discovery that the author of the guide, Rev. Samuel Hyman, was himself a grandson of Valentine Greatrakes. And the further coincidental discovery that Richie Musgrove, the flash Harry with the sports car who had once dated Luke's Dublin cousin Alva O'Leary, is descended from the ancient knightly family of Musgrove whose seat was three miles away at Coolderry and who is, most likely, the grandson of Sir Richard Musgrove,

High Commissioner to the Kingdom of Iraq from 1923 to 1929.

Looking up and out, what view is he afforded through the window?

  From a seated position and looking through the pane of glass at the intersection of the second horizontal row from the base of the window and the third vertical row from the left, his view is of the front lawn, the complete branch-span of the sycamore tree to the left, a rectangular grid of sky and Paddy the dog chasing a bird across the lawn in a run-jump-bark pattern. From a standing position he has a view of the far bank of the river, the oak trees on the town side, the east gable of the derelict building that was St Joseph's Industrial School, the spire of the Catholic church, the bell tower of the Protestant church, four or five rooftops on the main street petering out towards the sky as the street rises. To the west, on the wooded hill above the town, Clonduff House, its chimneys, roof apex and the top panes of the third-storey Georgian windows just visible above the tree line. Currently the seat of Sir Richard Blake, nephew of Sir John Blake who famously, along with his wife Alice, possessed two motors cars in 1921, one of which, replete with cocktail cabinet, was commandeered by the IRA during the War of Independence and never returned. Closer, beyond the lawn and the adjoining field, Luke has a view of the river surface, the copious oak foliage, the full afternoon sun giving the water a gold-green glow and a glimmery shimmery movement that puts him in mind of a phenomenon he once witnessed at evening time from a kayak at Castlehaven Bay in West Cork.

The phenomenon?

Bioluminescence. The chemical reaction of luciferin and luciferase that results in light-illuminated water. When daylight dimmed and a stroke of his paddle broke the surface and roused the plankton, a beautiful phosphorescent glow sparked into life. The darker it got, the brighter the glow, the liquid phosphorous sparking green and then lifting and shifting from unnameable shades of green to unnameable shades of blue, and back, like the multitudinous colours on the necks of wild water ducks. His heart lit up, his soul soared as he remembered the etymology of Lucifer as elucidated by Father Leo Moran, SJ, Latin teacher, in the corridor at Belvedere College one Friday morning during Lent – light-bringer, morning star, bringer of dawn, the devil before his fall – and then the downdraft as he contemplated the Luciferean glow in the cells of fish, fireflies and worms, in the tip of a match, on the skins of Hiroshimoans.

What two words each conferred with a pair of identical phonemes now escape his mouth in a whisper?

Lucy. Lucifer.

What sound comes from the far side of the door?

The urgent meowing of Lily the cat.

*   *   *

Does he admit her?

He crosses the room, opens the door and the cat dives past his legs across the floor towards the desk, pauses uncertainly, then jumps up on his chair.

What observation does he make?

From the loose swing of her udder-belly, she has just nursed her litter.

Why is the birth of this recent litter troubling?

The dilemma of whether to keep one or some or all of Lily's issue or find homes for one, some, or all troubles him.

What recollections of previous births are called up?

The last birth but one (under the bed in the blue room) when Lily signalled her imminent labour by loud meowing and a tail-lift display of a cylindrical-shaped plug of gelatinous mucous protruding from her vagina. Her second birth, two years ago, when he had five male friends down from Dublin for a weekend of partying and he woke at dawn on the Sunday morning, still drunk, to a warm wet sensation in his crotch. Believing he had urinated in his sleep, he made to rise. Then, feeling a slight movement and a weighted sensation, he reached down and touched something wet and live and crawling and he sprang upright in terror, convinced that his entrails had somehow exited his body. He pulled off the duvet and there sat a silent mass of moving fur and tiny limbs in black and white and faces with closed eyelids, and further down, Lily lodged in a v-shaped gap between his thighs, panting, her tiny tongue out, her terrified eyes fixed on him, in the throes of another delivery. He edged his legs further apart and remained there in a barely-breathing, pseudo-panting trance until her ordeal was over.

Why is he suddenly filled with remorse?

Because, despite his repeated resolve (repeated now again), he has neglected to have Lily spayed.

With what compensatory thought does he (a) comfort himself and (b) exonerate himself?

That the short memory of the pangs of birth almost universally avowed by human mothers might also apply to Lily and the joys of motherhood – nursing her kittens, witnessing their playful frolics – compensate for the hardships of pregnancy and birth.

What extra concession did he briefly grant Lily, following the birth of her second-last litter?

For a period of three weeks and two days he supplemented her tinned food with tasty morsels of roast chicken purchased at the hot food counter in SuperValu.

What disquieting feature did he discover as he removed the flesh from the carcasses of each cooked chicken?

Every single wing-bone in every single chicken was broken.

Why did this discovery distress him and compel him to cease for ever (to date) the purchase of chickens for consumption by his Lily or any other Lily, human or non-human?

He firstly surmised that the wing-bones were broken in the processing stage to facilitate easy packaging and/or to save space during storage, transportation or distribution. This initial supposition was swiftly replaced by his conviction that, at some point in their short miserable lives, in order to restrict movement and thwart flight in their confined cages, the chickens' wings were broken manually or mechanically.

What knowledge gives weight to this latter supposition?

The insider knowledge of standard production practices in chicken factories as relayed to him by Colin Doyle, Conor Mahon and Tom Carragher over the summer months in 1995 and 1996 when they worked on the production line at Clonduff Chickens; the account of the imagined life of a chick in a hatchery as relayed by a Nobel prize-winning author known for his compassion for animals in a lecture that Luke watched on YouTube approximately six months ago.

Practices such as?

Overcrowding, debeaking, the shredding of two-day-old chicks into paste.

Chicks are shredded?

Shredded, crushed, pulped, ground, grated, milled, mulled, pulverised. In the lecture the author gave an account of what happens after a batch of chicks are hatched out. Let us imagine a camera following them, the author said. On day two of their lives they are placed on a conveyor belt, on each side of which stand human minions who lift the chicks and turn them over to check the sex. Sexing the chicks, it's called. The female chicks are transferred to another conveyor belt behind the workers and sent on up the line. The camera homes in on one chick from the moment it is placed on the first belt, chirping happily among its peers like any baby species, the author tells us, moving along without a care in the world, and then *hey, what's this*, he's grabbed, picked up and turned over as human fingers part the yellow fluff between his legs. Instantly he's placed back on the belt, and the camera watches as he rights himself, gives himself a little shake, relieved after his first big adventure in the world, and then along he goes, happy and chirpy again until the belt suddenly plunges south and the chick is tipped over the edge and out of sight, like a canoeist going over a rapid. Except that our little friend is dropped into a motorized shredder and instantly shredded and ground into a paste, to be used later as an ingredient in animal feed.

What hypothetical book comes to mind?

The Book of Infamy, as expounded upon by another author (female, Polish, name forgotten) interviewed on BBC Radio 4's *Open Book* a few years ago, a book which, to the best of Luke's knowledge, does not yet exist. The author was travelling the world on a mission: taking photographs, collecting evidence, compiling reports, gathering excerpts from modern and ancient texts alike for inclusion in her work-in-progress which will be an exhaustive account of the crimes of man from the dawn of history to the present day. Nothing will be omitted, she said. It will be man's confessions.

Wishing to sit, what does Luke do?

He whooshes Lily off his chair, pours the milky-tea dregs from his mug onto the plate whereupon the liquid is instantly absorbed by the bread crust to the point of saturation. He places the plate on the floorboards beyond the perimeter of the rug, and watches Lily lapping up the milky-tea mush. When she is finished she sits back and washes her paws, jaws, neck, head, belly and backside, then moves to a sunny spot on the rug and basks in the flood of sunshine.

With a pen, paper and a concerted effort to neutralise distressing thoughts that are starting to surface, what list does Luke now compile?

A list of potential moneymaking enterprises, ideas and options.

List these moneymaking enterprises.
  – Let the house and grounds as a venue for weddings, conferences, yoga retreats, rock festivals, literary festivals.
  – Open a B&B business.
  – Give English grinds to Leaving Cert students.
  – Teach an evening course on *Ulysses*.

- Found a school, the Ardboe Academy for Excellence.
- Write articles on topics such as the move from the city to the country, the rural–urban divide, the paucity of public services in rural Ireland, the paucity of romance in rural Ireland, the poverty of small-town Ireland, the lives of men and boys in small-town Ireland, the fluidity of sexuality.
- Schools Guide to *Ulysses*.

To what does he now turn his attention?

To the copy of *Ulysses* propped open (at pages 776 and 777) on the bookstand.

What does the sight of *Ulysses*, or the mere thought of it, always provoke in him?

Evocations of home. Metaphorical home, repose of the soul. A longing for Bloom, for filial love, fellow feeling.

Has he read the novel, in consecutive pages, up to this point?

He has circled back and forth in a haphazard but sometimes chronological pattern. Since his first reading (haphazardly) in the second term of First Year English at UCD in 1997, during which he failed to complete the Cyclops, Oxen of the Sun and Circe episodes, he has, on many occasions, read random episodes in their entirety and certain (favoured) episodes repeatedly, chronologically, obsessively (Eumaeus, Ithaca and Penelope).

*   *   *

What pie-in-the-sky, moneymaking notion (listed above) related to *Ulysses* which he frequently entertains is he again reminded of?

The Ardboe Academy for Excellence aka The Ulysses Academy for Excellence at Ardboe. The idea of founding a private school with its own distinct curriculum and vision, whose student body would be drawn from the sons and daughters of forward-thinking parents unconcerned with CAO points, SAT scores, Baccalaureate results or arid, orthodox methodologies and whose curriculum would be devised using one source, *Ulysses*, a work of genius, as the base text from which myriad other texts will follow . . . has long been fermenting. (It has always galled him that the tepid little souls at the Department of Education have never seen fit to put Joyce on the secondary school English curriculum – an adaptation of 'The Dead' hardly counts – and, in his opinion, ninety per cent of *Ulysses* is perfectly suitable for young minds.) When all the leads, references, riddles and allusions of the novel are followed and all the texts containing those leads, references, allusions etc. are explored – through the fields of literature, mythology, music, maths, science, history, theology, philosophy, art, ethics, aesthetics, astronomy, biology, embryology, physics, psychology, the earth sciences, languages, politics, law, etc. – the waterfront is covered. Initially, a thorough, in-depth study of *Ulysses* would be required (he has commenced this task on many occasions), after which he would compile an index of all the topics and texts cited in the novel, subdivided into the classics, the humanities, the sciences, etc.; from this he would construct a diagram with branches and sub-branches and sub-sub-branches of topics before devising the course outlines and syllabus and writing the specifics of each area of study. One text would lead naturally to another in an ever-increasing ripple and everything – from Plato to pop art – would be accessed to ensure the finest, broadest, pupil-directed education is provided. As headmaster he would select his staff from the ranks of the brilliant, the brave and the eccentric (if John Kidd, the Joycean scholar who disappeared into thin air years ago, ever resurfaces Luke will do his damnedest to coax him to Ardboe). He would attract the brightest and the best students and would offer scholar-ships to the poor and the talented. His would be a vocation in the truest, oldest sense of the word and his school a centre for excellence of the kind about which enlightened people rhapsodise and dullards mock. He has the perfect premises – a fine country house on a hundred and fifty acres – for the endeavour. The Ardboe Academy for Excellence. Give me the boy and I will so I will.

What sudden illumination regarding his Joyce project does he now experience?

It comes to him with the force of an undoubtable and certifiable truth: that his Joyce project is not the much-dreamed-of but hopelessly unachievable book he has longed to write, but this – the Ardboe Academy for Excellence. Or the Ardboe Academy for Excellence Featuring Ulysses. What better way to pay homage to Joyce than to found a school in his honour and use his work and his brain to nourish the minds of future generations? And how had he not thought of this before?

What first surprised and amused him about Leopold Bloom?

That he relished the tang of porcine urine in a fried kidney.

What first moved him most about Bloom?

His nature: the sight of him feeding the gulls, his compassion for Mina Purefoy in her long labour, his concern for the starving Dedalus children and for Dante Riordan in her bath-chair, his memory of his dead son Rudy, his worry that when he eats a steak the eyes of the cow will pursue him through all eternity.

What similarities do Luke and Bloom share?

The years on earth, similar but not the same (Bloom's thirty-eight to Luke's thirty-four), the delight in the sensual life, the love of water, the weave of the mind, the ruminations, the pity of love, the jealousy of love, the downward slides into self-doubt and self-pity interspersed with moments of pride, indignation, illumination. The temperamental assonance: the ranking of kindness above all virtues, the abhorrence of cruelty. The loss of sons they never knew (most miscarried foetuses are male). Both have walked the corridors of the National Maternity Hospital, Holles Street. Both are aware they may be the last male in the family line. Both have fond memories of their fathers. Both are linked to the agricultural economy (Bloom was once a clerk at the

Dublin cattle market at Hanlon's Corner). Both are protective of young men and boys as evidenced by Bloom's concern for Stephen in Nighttown and by Luke's heartsickness for the thin, pale, hungry, fatherless youths who hang around the town and the used, abused, surplus-to-requirement boys in tracksuits who drift around city shopping centres and whose hurt eyes may pursue him through all eternity.

What else?

Both are womanly men, unafraid of their feminine side, unafraid of women's bodies or minds or emissions – taking delight in women's bodies, minds and emissions. Molly claims that Bloom – whose middle name is Paula – feels what a woman *is*. He even contemplates sewing the one-and a-half-inch fissure in Stephen's jacket after the Nighttown adventure. (A black mark against Bloom, however, is his view of women's 'deficient mental development' and his disdain towards Molly for her reluctance to read literature, but this, Luke thinks, should be interpreted as a symptom of a long marriage – which requires 'the mutual toleration of personal defects', as Bloom says – and its accompanying frustrations, such as Bloom's valiant attempts to get Molly to take up some intellectually challenging pursuits, rather than as evidence of misogyny.) Bloom thinks disparagingly of those men who think themselves 'wits' when they spout belittling and sexist remarks about women. He asserts the need for state-inspected and medically controlled male brothels for the clandestine satisfaction of women's erotic irritation. Both Bloom and Luke have gone so far as to fantasise about being a woman and being pregnant; they have celebrated female desire, seminal warmth, the preordained frangibility of the hymen; both have worshipped at that altar where the back changes name. In the realm of the everyday, both relish their food and despite giving much thought to and having great sympatico with the suffering of animals remain, to date, carnivorous. Both have a fondness for cats and water and the taking of baths (or showers). Both fantasise about the ideal life and ways to become financially independent. Once, driving through the Burren, Luke came upon what appeared to be the exact replica of the cottage Bloom envisioned as his dream home, causing him such mental arrest that he almost crashed. Both are idealists, visionaries, dedicated to rectitude, social justice, utopian dreams – evidenced in Bloom's desire to rid the world of poverty, avarice, international animosity, and in Luke's almost filial affection and protectiveness towards the lost youth of the town, his dream of starting a school, his campaigns against the construction of pylons and wind farms, his occasional thoughts of entering politics in order to effect change. Luke is certain that if he and Poldy were to write their manifestos for life – on politics, religion, art, music, literature, birth, death, sex, love, pleasure, fantasy, the sacred and the profane – their beliefs, ideas and strategies would be almost identical. On the issue of sexuality too there are intimations of overlap: was not Bloom's masculinity questioned, and did he not possess a surfeit of feminine plasms in the brain, and was he not suspected by the men of Dublin of being a repressed homosexual? And in the realm of science, does not Luke's interest in and fascination with the multiverse, quantum mechanics, the Higgs Boson, Elon Musk's SpaceX, his own nascent theories and notions as to the existence of a compound that makes up the code of everything – the nucleus of the nebula – neatly parallel Bloom's interest in involutions increasingly vast, in microbes and cells and infinitely divisible particles until nought nowhere is ever reached and the whatness of our whoness is never known, in his theory of alien possibility, his meditation on the stars, the ramifications of number and his elaborate calculations of $9^9x9^9x9^9$ which might bring man to the divine? Indeed such are the similarities of the soarings and rhapsodic episodes that lead both men to frequent illuminations that, in certain moments at the height of his own flights, Luke could swear that Bloom is his brother from another mother.

To what does Luke credit his frequent illuminations?

To a specific but unknown spot in the folds of his cerebral cortex where the numerical faculties nestle; to long hours spent in solitude, to certain moments in childhood spent observing his mother, inspecting specks of dust, rays of slanting sun, the grain of wood, the variations of emerald in various cats' eyes; to the moment he discovered, at age twelve, that time travel is consistent with the laws of physics and the consequent realisation that past events and past lives are not really past but can be revisited over and over; to his infatuation with the lives of great artists, musicians, physicists who, in moments of transcendence, enter an eternal realm of abstract forms, a Platonic heaven far from the ordinary reality we inhabit, from which they bring back their knowledge and insights.

In what ways are Bloom and Luke dissimilar?

Physically, Luke is taller and proportionately slenderer, carrying 11 stone 3 pounds on his 6 feet 1 inch frame as opposed to Bloom's 11 stone 4 pounds on his 5 feet 9½ inch frame; Bloom's greater girth of neck is evidenced in his collar size of 17 against Luke's 15½. Sartorially, Bloom is smarter and better groomed and while there hangs in Luke's wardrobe a Paul Smith suit, several designer shirts, ties, shoes, the Hubie Clark apparel from the US, a brown slim-fitting Vivienne Westwood suit he especially loves, and though, during his life in the city – most notably during his gay period – he revelled in a well-coiffed, well-groomed appearance, he acknowledges there is little call for self-grooming these days and he has, consequently, grown increasingly rakish. Temperamentally, Bloom is more disciplined, more measured, less prone to excess of impulse or appetite, less likely to rant about injustice or fantasise about violent revenge. Philosophically, Bloom believes the universe is infinite and fathomless, and while Luke also believes it is infinite, he thinks man is edging towards fathoming it. Educationally, Luke, a graduate, is better schooled, but Bloom, with his knowledge of maths and science, astrology and astronomy and enormous quantities of general knowledge of innumerable subjects – including saints' feast days, the cubic area of Roundwood reservoir, the precise times of sunrise and sunset five days in advance – is more learned. Epicurally, Luke has never relished the inner organs of either beast or fowl.

Does Luke suspect Bloom is a repressed homosexual? Or a bisexual? What about Stephen? Or Joyce himself?

When younger, Luke harboured such or similar suspicions and doubts about all three men. Now he views Stephen as accepting of homosexual desire and attraction as part of his own and every man's nature, as is Bloom, though not explicitly. As was Joyce himself: nothing that was human was alien to him. Out of the crooked timber of humanity no straight thing was ever made. Joyce showed no signs of homosexual panic or, indeed, practice. The love between men is implicit and is everywhere evident in his work.

What character traits or attributes of Stephen's – in either *Portrait* or *Ulysses* – does Luke, to a greater or lesser extent, admire or find moving?

He admires to a greater extent Stephen's genius, his erudition, his exhaustive and enviable knowledge of literature, history, languages, theology, philosophy, psychology, philology, astrology, esoteric teachings, the Gospels and the finer points of Church doctrine and dogma; his longing to understand life and love in an intellectual sense; his full and fully-fledged renunciation of the Church after the full and fully-fledged devotion to the Church of his early youth; his continuous worship at the altar of female flesh, drawn to the swoon of sin and suffering; his intense personality. The life of his mind. His mystical elements, his thoughtful meditations, his creative impulse, his ability to read the divine signature in the snotgreen sea. Rare moments of self-deprecation too, remembering the books he was going to write containing his deeply deep epiphanies on green oval leaves, to be sent in the event of his death to the great libraries of the world, including Alexandria. Luke admires to a (far) lesser extent Stephen's immaturity, his (mostly) selfish disregard for his hungry sisters, his enormous ego, his precocious, brittle self, his bumptious, arrogant self, his pompous, sore-loser style of argument. Luke is moved by Stephen's fretful heart, his sensitive, shame-wounded soul, his agenbite of inwit, his susceptibility to the word *foetus*. His fear of thunder, his fragile self. His memory of his mother. His fears for his sister — *She is drowning*. His tears for himself, alone in the rain on the top of the Howth tram.

Who does Molly remind him of?

His mother. The cat that got the cream. The Queen of Sheba. Joyce, the womanly man. Himself, the womanly Luke.

To what wistful pondering does Luke occasionally succumb?

He often ponders on the activities of the residents of No. 7 Eccles Street on the morning of 17 June 1904 and wonders whether Poldy's uncharacteristic request for break-fast in bed the previous night might indicate a new accretion of authority, of potency even. Poldy might, on waking, find the sole of Molly's foot beat up against his face. He might sniff her toes, finger her instep, her fallen arch. Run a hand up her plump calf, around the back of her knee, up her thigh to her plumpen rumpen lumpen backside. And behold, a new dawn might herald at No. 7 Eccles Street.

What errors, issues or inconsistencies in *Ulysses* perplex or indeed irritate Luke?

Why does Bloom, at thirty-eight, seem so old – old enough for Stephen to pronounce him 'a profound ancient male'? Why is Moses Dlugacz, a Jewish butcher, selling pork kidneys? How long can a man carry a potato in his pocket before it rots? Why is Deasy, the headmaster of a Dalkey boys' school, writing a letter on foot and mouth disease in cattle? Why does Joyce say that the priest kneels when he means genuflects? Why does he write sweat-pea for sweet-pea and call a tap a faucet? Why does he call the Ascot Gold Cup a handicap race when even the dogs in the street know it's not? Why does it take four minutes for Bloom to climb the back stairs from his basement kitchen in 7 Eccles Street to the hall-door level? How can Stephen *recline* against the area railings of 7 Eccles Street *and* simultaneously have a view into the kitchen? What possessed Joyce to situate a bunch of rowdy men in a room in the National Maternity Hospital at ten o'clock at night drinking beer, eating sardine sandwiches and spouting lewd remarks while down the corridor several Dublin women are in the throes of labour? But by far the most baffling question is how, at the end of the night, on the walk from Beresford Place to Eccles Street (via Gardiner Street, Mountjoy Square, Temple Street North), a route that Luke knows well and estimates at fifteen to twenty minutes at normal pace and which Google Maps put at twenty minutes (and which would surely take no more than thirty to forty minutes at a slow and dawdling pace), can Bloom and Stephen, even allowing for 'interruptions of halt', possibly discuss – no, *deliberate on* – at least twenty subjects of substantial conversational heft, i.e. music, literature, Ireland, Dublin, Paris, friendship, women, prostitution, diet, the influence of gaslight on the growth of paraheliotropic trees, corporation bins, the Roman Catholic church, ecclesiastical celibacy, the Irish nation, Jesuit education, careers, the study of medicine, the past day, the influence of the pre-Sabbath, Stephen's collapse? Average per topic time: one minute. *And*, concurrent with these subjects, Bloom also privately recalls similar subjects discussed with other friends on previous nocturnal perambulations. *Impossible!*

Why is he doubly sceptical of these 'errors'?

Because '*A man of genius makes no mistakes. His errors are volitional and are the portals of discovery.*'

Has Luke located any of the portals?

He has not. Yet.

What surprises Luke about Joyce?

That he never visited ancient Greece.

Was he surprised by Bloom's visit to Bella Cohen's brothel?

No. Bloom is a sensualist, as Joyce himself was. As Luke is. In any case, he was there primarily to look after Stephen.

* * *

Has he, Luke, ever frequented a house of ill repute?

At the age of seventeen, during a free two-hour period on a school trip to Amsterdam in March 1995, he lost his virginity to a prostitute in a brothel on Bloedstraat. Debbie. Mixed race. Old enough to be his mother. Come for mamma. Wait wait good boy. Afterwards he felt a surge of what he thought was love for her. He told no one, ever. He occasionally thinks of her. She might be retired by now, providing a phone or online sex service. He wonders why they do it. No, he knows: money, rent, mouths to feed. Poor women and girls. Riddled with the pox in the old days. The way they're mentioned in the biographies of famous men, as if they were sub-human, as if they weren't daughters or sisters or mothers. Graham Greene's list of prostitutes. Treated as vermin, as if *they* were the cause of the pox. Poor girls. Biddy the Clap and Cunty Kate. No word of their suffering. Joyce himself, from the age of fourteen, a regular frequenter of the kips. Metaphysics in Mecklenburg Street.

How did Luke react to the discovery that Joyce was syphilitic?

With devastation. It altered everything: how he saw Bloom (with greater understanding), how he saw Joyce (with greater compassion), how he read *Ulysses* (with greater sorrow). He is haunted by two images of Joyce: the beautiful, innocent, half-past-six boy entering Clongowes Wood in 1888, and the frail old man groping around a dark room in 7 rue Valentin in 1939. He spent hours online reading about syphilis, studying the grotesque images of the disease – the penile chancres and discharge, the scabrous fissures in unwashed crotches, the rashes, the incontinence, the impotence. Limp father of thousands, languid floating flower. The more he read the more convinced he was of the evidence for Joyce's infection, and the deeper his sorrow grew for the man.

What evidence?

The daily afflictions: the failing eyes, the abdominal cramps, the joint pain, the bad teeth. Then later, the creative euphoria, electrocution by divine fire, the breeze of madness. Other symptoms too: Beckett the bastard told Ellmann that Joyce wore two newspapers inside his trousers. He was treated with Galyl, an arsenic and phosphorous compound patented by Dr A. Mouneyrat and commonly prescribed for syphilis before the discovery of penicillin. And the books are crawling with the disease – it's embedded and encoded in labyrinthine references in *Ulysses*. Bloom in all likelihood had it too – he also visited prostitutes in his youth – and there are indications that he too is ill. And Bloom and Joyce are both obsessed with the body, with morbus germs and contamination. So many geniuses, all male, infected . . . Van Gogh, Beethoven, Oscar Wilde, Baudelaire. He wonders if the pox unleashed the brilliance or if the brilliant flocked to the pox, more than half in love with easeful death.

How, in Luke's opinion, did the knowledge of his syphilitic condition affect Joyce?

It was, Luke is certain, the single greatest presence, the

gravest event, the biggest grief, in Joyce's mature adult life; the shaper and signifier of everything – his thoughts, his work, his outer life, his secret inner life. It preoccupied and consumed him, spreading its tentacles into every corner of his psyche. Riddled with shame and guilt, constantly awaiting the re-emergence of the sinister signs and symptoms of the illness, constantly fearing madness, always guarding the secret. Worst of all he believed it to be the cause of Lucia's madness. I have syphilis, Pappy, she said to him one day, the inexplicable access of the mad to the truth. As if in compensation – or atonement – for the sins of his youth he lived a quiet, reserved life in Zurich and Paris, never countenancing bad language or vulgarity, dining nightly with his little family in Fouquet's and shunning the lifestyle the avant-garde expected of him. Despite his avowed rejection of the Church he went to the annual Holy Week services – he the eternal penitent and the Catholic guilt impossible to expunge. He ate blackberry jam because Christ's crown of thorns was made from blackberry briars. From what he has read about *Finnegans Wake*, Luke suspects syphilis was the driving force of that novel, suffused and threaded as it is with oblique references, messages and admissions of the disease, the writing of it an act of sublimation, a straining for a cure, a metaphorical fix, as if he was trying to confess and right his wrongs, purge his soul, seek forgiveness for the damage done.

What thought makes Luke smile?

The thought of some PhD student presenting to his or

her professor a thesis proposal entitled 'Thank Syphilis for *Ulysses*'.

Why does Luke think himself lucky?

Because it's on the rise again and he, Luke, an MSM, could've been riddled. Maeve had a dose of thrush once; he had to anoint his member with ointment. No cup overfloweth.

Directing his gaze out the window, what posture does he adopt?

He straightens up, flexes his facial muscles by opening wide his mouth, first vertically, then horizontally, closes his left eye and holds that position, then reopens it and closes his right eye. The purpose: to check for slack or paralytic flesh in his face; to check the status of the vision in his left eye whose sight he is certain is deteriorating. A word, *parallax*, comes to mind. He opens his laptop and Googles the word.

The results?

Out of a total of over 32 million results, and after trawling through several pages, he chooses — owing to the attractive and vaguely familiar title — a link to an excerpt from 'The Story of the Heavens' by Sir Robert Ball:

We must first explain clearly the conception which is known to astronomers by the name of parallax; for it is by parallax that the distance of the sun, or, indeed, the distance of any other celestial body, must be determined. Let us take a simple illustration.

Stand near a window from whence you can look at buildings, or the trees, the clouds, or any distant objects. Place on the glass a thin strip of paper vertically in the middle of one of the panes. Close the right eye, and note with the left eye the position of the strip of paper relatively to the objects in the background. Then, while still remaining in the same position, close the left eye and again observe the position of the strip of paper with the right eye. You will find that the position of the paper on the background has changed. As I sit in my study and look out of the window I see a strip of paper, with my right eye, in front of a certain bough on a tree a couple of hundred yards away; with my left eye the paper is no longer in front of that bough, it has moved to a position near the outline of the tree. This apparent displacement of the strip of paper, relatively to the distant background, is what is called parallax.

What conclusion regarding this result does he arrive at?

That this definition of parallax is not now the one he wants; that what he wants is a more symbolic or metaphoric, or even simpler definition. That he can consult an online dictionary or trawl through the other results to find a more favoured definition. That he can find the same word with a thousand different faces. That this surfeit of instant online information feeds a certain need, a hunger, but such instant gratification leaves him unsatisfied, like eating fast food or wearing cheap clothes, because such easy acquisition of knowledge lacks the awe, the pleasure of serendipity, the sense of award that real learning brings. He could learn Latin and Greek online, become proficient at astronomy but he knows something would be missing: the connection, the immersion, the thoroughness and warmth and civilising effect that real-life interaction with learned teachers brings. This thought similar, he thinks, to the belief he once held that babies born using IVF – humans incubated in test tubes – were missing out on something essential, the soul maybe, in the act of creation.

What urge is he fighting?

The urge to log on to his Gmail account and check if Ruth Mulvey has emailed.

How does he abate this urge?

He lights a cigarette, takes two drags, leaves it on the ashtray and then types the words 'world news March 1965' into Google. From millions of results he reads two articles, the first on the slaughter in Selma, Alabama, on Sunday, 7 March, the second on the civil rights' march led by Martin Luther King from Selma to Montgomery on Tuesday, 9 March. He searches again, typing the words 'Ireland news March 1965'. There is no mention of a breach of promise court case. Among the more interesting results is the report that, under the new Vatican II rules, Masses were said in the vernacular for the first time in Ireland that month.

In order to occupy his mind and so desist from scouring the internet for material related to Ellen and Mulvey's court case, what does he do?

For an unspecified number of minutes or hours-and-minutes he reads three segments – pages 776 to 789, pages 818 to 846, pages 862 to 867 – in the penultimate episode of *Ulysses*.

What excerpts does he favour and/or consider exceptionally clever or witty?

Bloom's account of the journey of Dublin's municipal water as it flows down from Roundwood reservoir through subterranean aqueducts and pipeage to Stillorgan reservoir and onwards through a system of relieving tanks, weirs and street pipes into the tap in the kitchen of 7 Eccles Street; his meditation on the constellation of stars, the likelihood of the inhabitability of planets other than Earth by an anatomically different race of beings to human, and the possibility of the moral redemption of said race by a redeemer; the description of his fantasy home – a thatched two-storey dwellinghouse of southerly aspect with an orchard, tennis court, shrubbery, rockery, summer glasshouse etc. (the replica of which Luke spotted in the Burren); proof that Bloom advocated, instigated and supported programmes of rectitude since his earliest youth; the reason for his smile if he had smiled as he entered the matrimonial bed; the justification for the retribution he would hypothetically mete out to the matrimonial violator who had earlier occupied the matrimonial bed.

By what is Luke startled?

By a heavy thud on the window, the sound of an object unexpectedly colliding with the glass. Judging it a soft-bodied living creature by the sound of the impact and the instant painful sensation (which he now concludes must be mirror-touch synaesthesia) gripping his own body, he stands, leans over the desk, peers out. Lying on the gravel about thirty inches from the wall and at an angle of approximately forty-five degrees from the windowsill, is the body of a bird, a baby tit lying on its side, its legs horizontal to the ground, the pale down of its underbelly ruffling lightly in the breeze. He watches and waits, his fingers a-tremble, hoping it has just knocked itself out briefly. Sighing audibly in an effort to trick his body into shedding its sympathetic pain and his mind into asserting a robust masculine nonchalance, he draws back from the window, crosses the room, walks to the front hall and exits the front door. He bends to the bird. The eyes are open but the bird is dead. As he considers various means of removing it (the shovel from the fireside companion set in the drawing room being the first and favoured option), its eyelids blink. A wing twitches. A foot stirs. The bird is trying to die. Or trying to rise. He strokes its fur, lifts it gently, propping it upright on its belly-body. The bird sways, then the whole body shivers almightily. From the corner of his eye Luke registers Paddy's approach. Another shiver, a wing twitch, an eye blink. The head turns twenty to thirty degrees to the left, eyes blinking urgently. Luke stands, turns, grabs Paddy by the collar and hauls him roughly across the gravel, around the corner to the old kitchen, then pushes him inside and bolts the door.

*   *   *

And the tit?

On his return the tit is still propped on its belly, head turning right and left, more alert. As he watches, it rises shakily on thin legs and turns until the tail is where the head was and vice versa, and it turns again and seems to be looking at him. He steps away. Another movement – so swift that he barely catches it – and an upward motion and a diagonal flight across his sight path and the tit is gone, out over the lawn.

How does Luke occupy himself for the evening?

At 6.20 p.m. he switches on the hot water immersion. He brings a bowl of dry dog food soaked in water out to the old kitchen for Paddy, refills his water bowl at the tap in the yard, and spends a few minutes rolling a tennis ball across the floor towards him. He returns to the house, re-emerges with a tin of cat food and spoons out the contents onto the ground in three little mounds as the cats swarm around his legs. He fills two old fertiliser bags with logs, places them on the wheelbarrow and wheels them to the front door. From the flowerbeds, right of the front door, he breaks off four stems of Salvia and pulls five Shasta daisies. He carries the flowers inside, arranges them in a glass vase with water and leaves them on the hall table.

As he stands admiring the flowers, by what is he again startled?

By the ringing of his phone.

*　　*　　*

The caller?

Ruth.

Do they talk?

Yes. She, in a state of distress, tells him she knew nothing of her father's engagement to Ellen until she read his email. She then called her mother, who confirmed her knowledge of her father's engagement, that her father had not loved 'the woman' and that 'the woman' had sued him for breach of promise. Her mother knew nothing about anonymous letters or rumours of a child and is now very upset. She finds it hard to believe Ruth's father would behave like that — as indeed Ruth does. My father was a kind man, she says. There must be more to this than meets the eye. She pauses, and then twice says his name urgently, *Luke, Luke*, and asks if he is there.

Luke's response?

His hand grips the phone tighter. He takes a deep breath and asks if she read the documents he emailed her.

Her reply?

She did. She says her father must have believed what was written in the anonymous letters. He must have had reason to believe they were genuine and their contents true.

What is Luke tempted to do?

To hang up.

* * *

Does he?

No. Instead he reminds Ruth that *none* of the contents of the letters were true, they were all fabricated, that Ellen begged her father to believe *her* and trust *her* and not some anonymous letter-writer. Ruth says this happened almost fifty years ago, these were other people's lives, other people's mistakes. He counters – not other people, your father. What he did to Ellen marked her life for ever. Your father, he says, went on to have a life, he went on to marry and have a family.

What happens then?

Back and forth they go. He says, she says. Tempers flare. The gulf widens.

Relay the final moments of the conversation.

'Why do I feel like I'm being judged,' she says, 'and punished for something I didn't do? I'm being punished for the supposed sins of my father.'

'You're not being punished. This is hard for me too. But I have to think of Ellen now. I cannot desert her. I cannot betray her.'

'Betray her? What about me? Is this it? You always talk about being open and honest with each other and now I'm shocked at how *final* you sound, how unfair and judgmental!'

'And I'm shocked at how little compassion – how little mercy – you have for an old woman who was put through hell by your father! Put yourself in her shoes for a minute, Ruth. Then put yourself in mine.'

And then?
He hangs up, switches off his phone and tosses it on the chaise longue. Angry, shocked, rattled, he sits looking from him for an unmeasured period of time.

As the anger abates, what happens?
Tears fall.

On what does he ponder?
On the word 'mercy'. On Ruth. On the supposed sins of her father. On the loss of her. On the image of her at the other end of the phone. On her suffering. On her mother's suffering. On the balance sheet of love. On the charge sheet of feeling. On what makes one kind of love more worthy than another. On what places romantic love, in the eyes of society, above the love of an elderly relative. On how the hands of fate can reach across fifty years and stick a knife in him and her and her and her. On the countless difficulties of relationships. On the merits of a solitary life. On the greater possibility of living a good life alone. On the greater possibility of living a spiritual life alone. On how best to occupy himself for the evening and banish from his mind all thoughts of a single, solitary fateful future.

*   *   *

How does he occupy himself for the evening?

At 7.35 p.m. he enters the drawing room, removes the ashes from the ash pan, arranges wood on the grate, switches on the lamp over the piano, stands at the mahogany cabinet for several minutes considering the purple velvet case containing his grandmother's set of apostle spoons, the master and the twelve, sitting snugly inside. He goes upstairs and, in the bathroom, shaves, showers, shampoos his hair. After drying himself, he flosses and brushes his teeth, trims his nose hair, clips his toenails. He enters the bedroom and dresses in pale blue boxer shorts, a brown silk shirt, jeans and brown leather moccasins.

Occupied thus, on what does he ruminate?

On the pleasures of the night ahead. On the probability that Paddy will object to his early lock-in by barking. On the glow of the evening sun on his skin as he dresses and on the foresight of the nineteenth-century architect to situate dual-aspect windows in this room. On the heredity law that states it takes three generations to make a gentleman. On the myth that it takes three generations to lose a fortune. On the ruthless forces that drive the universe. On the swampy nature of the human mind. On the river capture. On the tsunami that knocked the earth six and a half inches off its axis and moved Japan four metres closer to the United States. On the realisation that *Ulysses* is probably the only book, Bloom the only character, and Joyce the only author whose company he would never willingly relinquish. On the likelihood that Joyce named his daughter for St Lucy, the patron saint of eyesight, and not Lucia di Lammermoor, who went mad. On the prevalence of syphilis among geniuses and the likelihood that the rogue bacterium gnawed at their brains and lured them into deeper and darker recesses of the unconscious from where they unearthed deeper and darker contents than they would ever have unearthed *sans* spirochete. On the surprising drop in temperature in the drawing room for this time of year as night falls. On his failed attempt to read even the first chapter of the Quran. On the imp of the perverse. On the unwelcome coincidence and provenance of the Mulvey name with the other Mulvey and his lingual penetration under the Moorish wall. On the different tempos of time and how gravity warps time – how, for instance, if one lives on a ground-floor apartment one ages slightly less rapidly than the neighbour in the penthouse; and why it is estimated that by the age of eight we have, subjectively, lived two-thirds of our lives. On the predilection for and the preponderance of American catchphrases, coined words and acronyms such as 24/7, my bad, natch, OMG, FYI, ATM, LMAO. On the phonetic, syllabic and rhythmic assonance between the acronyms for his personality type according to the Myers-Briggs typology test (INFJ) and the Latin abbreviation for King of the Jews (INRI). On the period some years ago when, after reading all the novels of John McGahern and Edna O'Brien, he was convinced the two writers had conducted a clandestine love affair and the evidence of the affair was embedded in cryptic passages and codes in their novels. On his youthful intimations that he possessed within him, among other gifts, the germ of a great scientific truth – a sign or formula or compound containing the key of life, the code to everything – and that this formula was ordinary and simple – simpler than Pi or $E=mc^2$ or the Fibonacci sequence – and close at hand, already existing in nature, something right under our noses – carbon or iron or zinc, a nutrient in clay or some common fungus. On the moments when he was convinced he was approaching this scientific breakthrough, and it was only a matter of time before the answer was dropped down to him or arrived in sleep and he would wake up, and reveal the code of everything to everyone.

Does he still believe in the existence of such a key or code to everything?

He has a hunch it is in water. That the simple hydrogen-oxygen compound in its purest, uncontaminated state contains the nucleus within which lies the quantum code for everything – the key to life and matter. For a time he became briefly enthralled with the experiments of Masaru Emotu, who claimed that water molecules are affected by human words, thoughts and intentions, and that, when frozen, water forms beautiful or ugly crystals depending on whether beautiful or ugly, positive or negative words, thoughts and intentions are focused on it. These claims were subsequently discredited for lacking scientific publication, peer review and scientific provability.

Pseudoscience and quackery, then, no scientific evidence to support his hunch?

No. *However,* according to *New Scientist,* researchers at the Max Planck Institute in Mainz, Germany, have since discovered that the structural memory of water persists on a picosecond timescale, a picosecond being one thousandth of one billionth of a second. If water retains traces or memories or records or resonances − or whatever water's equivalents to traces, memories, records and resonances are − of what it has passed through or of what has passed through it, then who knows what else it retains, or what else may yet be discovered about water and its properties.

What, in his opinion, caused his youthful intimations to dim and pass and what attendant emotions did their passing give rise to?

The dimming is due partly to the speed with which theoretical physics, experimental physics, biophysics, particle physics, astrophysics, quantum physics, molecular physics and all the biologies have advanced in the second half of his life to date, his copious reading of theories of the multiverse, string theory, supersymmetry, the phenomenon of quantum entanglement and quantum spin, the search for the god particle in a suburb outside Geneva, and the fact that what once was science fiction has now become science − all of which sate his curiosity and provide answers to questions which previously triggered the intimations. Due partly too to his own circumstances, the course of his own life and his familial responsibilities. The attendant emotions: disappointment and occasional resentment that he has not been part of the scientific community and such scientific investigations; relief, because of a niggling concern about his mental health due to the fact that those soarings – of which the intimations and illuminations were part thereof – came perilously close to the deranging altitudes to which manias ascend; a humbling admission that the unravelling of nature's secrets will take place in minds far superior to his own; feelings of conflict due to the belief that, as the scientific world moves ever closer to explaining everything, mankind may be slipping closer to extinction, that man is nearly done in this existence and the dissolution of the self is at hand; the belief that there will be *nothing left* for him to reveal, and no place left where he can soar or shine, has led him to feel or possess or become, in recent years, a flattened spirit, a loss of self-esteem, a growing bitterness, a private resentment, a fragile ego, an approximate man.

By what are these ruminations periodically interrupted?

By the report of a not-too-distant chainsaw while he dresses in the bedroom. By the sight of the open latches on the wooden trunk at the end of the bed. By a palate salivating and a tongue blue mouldy for the want of red wine.

Into what further ruminations or actions do these latter interruptions propel him?

The report of the chainsaw causes him momentary sorrow for the grief of the surviving trees. The sight of the open latches of the wooden trunk provoke in him the urge to view the wedding gown in its transparent protector inside the trunk.

*   *   *

Does he succeed in mastering this latter urge?

He does not. He opens the trunk, lifts out the white silk brocade gown, removes the protector, drapes the gown across the bed, sniffs the fabric and opens the pearl buttons at the back. He considers trying to convert the cost of the gown ($450 in 1962) to today's money but realises that such an attempt would, without the use of a calculator to compound the interest, be futile. He removes his shirt and jeans, lifts the heavy gown over his head and shoulders, pushes his arms into the sleeves and pulls and tugs until the ample skirt and tulle underskirt flow from a point approximately three inches above his waist and the hem is approximately four inches off the floor. He then turns and views himself in the mirror of the wardrobe door. As he adjusts the wardrobe door to get a better view he catches his reflection in the mirror over the fireplace and, in the motion, his own image is doubled, tripled, quadrupled – multiple, infinite Lukes in a wedding gown caught in the act of adjusting infinite doors in one fluid flowing infinite motion. Light-headed and a little dizzy, he puts a hand out to steady himself and the hand comes towards him as if to greet himself. The mathematics of turbulence, he thinks. No, the mathematics of quantum mechanics, where all possible outcomes do happen, each in its own universe, and every road is travelled and a particle can be both *here* or *there* precisely because it is here in one universe and there in another. A profusion of parallel universes and in each universe, right now, there is a copy of him in his wedding gown. For an instant he is trapped in the mirrors, falling towards the man in the white gown as the man in the white gown falls towards him. Vertiginous in mind and body he pauses, stands very still. He puts his hand to the wardrobe door and slowly, carefully, moves it back so that the fireplace mirror is out of view and the multiple Lukes are out of view and he can return to his singular self. He sighs deeply, smiles at himself, then joins his hands in a bridal pose. He twirls, pouts, preens, then runs his hands over his chest and his make-believe breasts. *Do you Lukey-Luke-Luke . . . Tippy two, tippy tea, tippy ta-ta too . . . till death do you part?*

By what means does he prevail over the salivating palate?

By hastily casting off the wedding gown, throwing on his own clothes, hurrying along the landing, down the stairs, along the back hall into the kitchen. By uncorking a bottle of Campo Viejo Tempranillo Reserva, filling three-quarters of a large glass, taking a slug of it, and feeling immediately his own return, his palate soothed and his equilibrium restored.

What meditations occupy Luke during the preparation of his evening meal and with what edible, audible and olfactory pleasures does he accompany these meditations?

Meditations: on the taste of altar wine as first experienced from the Holy Communion chalice at Sunday Mass in St Anne's Church, Clonduff, circa June 1986; on his childhood fascination with the grotesquery of transubstantiation and, at age nine, his re-enactment with Lucy, aged eleven, of the Last Supper (preceded by the wedding feast at Cana) using, as props, a Waterford Crystal wine glass, diluted Ribena, discs of Barron's sliced white pan and a yellow plastic bucket half full of water; on whether he should immediately uncork another bottle of wine so that it has ample time to breathe before being imbibed, or better still – because uncorking does nothing to aerate the wine – decant or double decant; on the pleasure of altar wine for an alcoholic priest; on the problem of altar wine for a recovering alcoholic priest; on Bloom's reluctance to elaborate on the futility of calculating the trillions of billions of millions of imperceptible molecules on a single pinhead and progressing to the nought nowhere that is never reached. Accompaniments: three handfuls of Manhattan salted peanuts intermittently scooped from the packet and shot from the palm of his hand into his open mouth. Two additional glasses (large) of wine. The first (and most favoured) movement of Keith Jarrett's *The Köln Concert*. The aroma of sautéed onions and garlic, golden fried, sea-salt-sprinkled potatoes; the sound of three small lamb chops being seared on a hot pan.

What informational titbit regarding the application of heat to protein first conveyed to him in biology class in his first year at St Mary's Secondary School does he now recall?

The application of heat to protein causes the protein to coagulate as evidenced when a raw egg or raw meat meets a hot surface.

How does he eat the lamb chops, the sautéed onions and garlic, the sea-salted, golden-fried potatoes?

With knife, fork, additional sea salt, additional wine, and relish.

What thoughts, memories and images are triggered by his evening meal?

The Sunday lunches of his childhood years, comprising roast beef with homemade gravy, or leg of lamb with shop-bought mint sauce whose sharp acidic tang made him shudder. That the misery of man escapes when he drinks. That Kafka's grandfather was a butcher. The image of the first ever blooding of man, the first hominoid or *Homo erectus* or *Homo sapiens* that ingested, digested and assimilated the first morsel of flesh – animal, fish, fowl, insect or worm; the weight of it, raw, on the tongue, the ferrous tang, the texture of tissue and sinew taut in the teeth. The journey of the masticated meat down the hominoidinal gullet, the action of hominoidinal enzymes in the hominoidinal intes-tines on the meat, the digestion and incorporation of one creature into another, flesh into flesh, the laying down of one set of DNA on another, the commencement of new epigenetic signalling as animal impressions mingle with early human instincts. Millennia of incorporation. He belches, sighs, pours more wine. *Incorporate.* He says the word aloud. *Corp.* Irish, French, Latin, all the same. With the fingers of his right hand he pinches the plumpest part of his left forearm and watches the released flesh spring back into place. Tissue, sinew. *Sin-you.* Decades of meat consumption. Well-blooded by now, the animal residue amassed in his cells. He bends his head and smells his left armpit. Policemen sweating Irish stew into their shirts – funny old Poldy! He sits back and attempts to calculate the ratio of human-to-animal molecules extant in his body, or, easier, the Luke-to-bovineovineporcineavine ratio.

What Luke-to-bovineovineporcineavine ratio does he arrive at?

With a current body weight of 11 stone 7 pounds (73kg) and assuming that he supped solely on milk for the first year of life and, notwithstanding the fact that he probably comes from one of the greatest meat-eating families in the Sullane valley if not in the entire province, consumption of meat in his infancy was negligible, so he commences the FCC (Flesh Consumption Count) from the age of four years and takes the daily recommended meat allowance of four ounces (100g) of meat (bovine, ovine, porcine or avine) as his benchmark unit and uses this unit as a (modest) measure of his daily meat consumption over the course of thirty years, and allowing that between 40 to 60 per cent of food (herbivoric, carnavoric and omnivoric) is assimilated (depending on genetic factors, physical activity, individual variable basal metabolic, thermogenetic and excretory rates) and remembering that the higher the carnivoric content the greater the assimilation rate, and acknowledging that the majority of food is either converted to fuel to run the metabolic and physiological activities that sustain life, tissue building and maintenance, or stored as fat, and that the tenth rule of trophic assimilation states that only 10 per cent of organic matter is stored as flesh, and not forgetting that the body mass of an average healthy man comprises approximately 62 per cent water, 16 per cent protein, 16 per cent fat, 6 per cent minerals, >1 per cent carbohydrates and other nutrients . . . he attempts to hold these rapidly accumulating facts, figures and variables in mental pyramidic arrangement while simultaneously attempting a mental pyramidic tally . . . and soon concludes that such mind-boggling holding, arranging and tallying (while also feeling the seductive lull of the Tempranillo) is next to nigh impossible, at which point he reaches across the table for a pen and a sheet of paper and, taking a calculator out of the table drawer, proceeds to calculate as follows:

Consumption: One (100g) unit of meat daily x 30 years = 1,095,000 g = 1,095kg

Assimilation: 50% (at an aver. of 40–60% assimilation rate) of 1,095kg = 547.5kg

Stored as flesh: 10% = 54.75kg

Divided by 30 years = 1.825kg assimilated

Body weight: 73kg

Assimilated meat as % of body weight = 1.825 ÷ 73 x 100 = 2.5

He concludes that the Luke-to-bovineovineporcineavine ratio is 40:1. He is 2.5 per cent animal.

Why is he sceptical of this result?

Because his calculation does not take into account (his ignorance of) the complexities of chemical digestion and the anabolic, catabolic, deaminatory and myriad other functions of protein and amino acids; because of his scant knowledge of the coupling of intercellular water and active metabolic processes or the coupling of mammalian stress systems and human gut biomes, or his limited knowledge of intestinal enzymes, intestinal flora, the functions and processes of nutrient absorption, human metabolic rates and the factors affecting these (such as physical activity, health of the organs, emotional state, body toxins, body temperature and food temperature at times of consumption); because of his failure to apply deferential calculus to the calculation; because of his inability to adhere to the scientific method of calculation; because the figure arrived at (or a more accurate figure that might be arrived at using deferential calculus) takes no account of lateral gene transfer, epigenetic inheritance, epimutations (particularly meat-related epigenetic changes), or of the marriage of flesh unto flesh and instinct unto instinct and the thirty years' accumulation of animal essence in his essence and animal soul in his soul; because the first time Gandhi ate meat he heard the lamb he had eaten bleating in his belly.

Has he ever abstained from eating meat or considered the benefits of routine fasting?

In his early childhood, as a result of his parents' feeble attempt to respect the last vestiges of Catholicism still extant in them, the family half-heartedly abstained from meat on Ash Wednesdays and Good Fridays. In 2004 he observed the twenty-four-hour Lenten fast with the Belvedere boys, during which he developed an acute headache that rendered him half blind and fully mute. At the end of the fast he experienced a brief feeling of elation followed by a profound – and again brief – sense of peace. While he retains a great admiration for those who lead disciplined ascetic lives, he suspects his own innate nature veers towards the gluttonous, the conger eel, making him an unlikely candidate for ascetic practices. Rachid, who fasted Ramadan annually, ardently advocated the benefits of fasting for the body, mind, and soul – and to ensure a place in Heaven. Luke watched the film *Hunger* three times. After one viewing he read about the process of ketosis and though the thought of his body eating itself from the inside out repulsed him, the knowledge that fasting helps repair hair follicles temporarily interested him.

What theories concerning mankind's evolution interest Luke and what separate theories has he himself hatched?

Bio-techies and Astronomers Royal alike agree that (a) Darwinian evolution is drawing to a close; (b) Man is on the precipice of a great anthropogenic catastrophe; and (c) the post-human era is fast approaching, when computers will augment our brains and out-think and out-do mankind so that the shackles of body and blood are finally loosed, allowing the human species to diverge into artificially enhanced, intelligent cybernetic organisms. *However,* as we await our fleshless progeny and if, in the interim, man hasn't already boiled himself to death through global warming or exterminated himself in a major environmental perturbation or so psychically damaged himself by intolerable stress, pervasive surveillance and inhuman violence that his soul is corroded beyond redemption and his very humanity is compromised beyond repair, Luke theorises that he – we – will either (a) eat ourselves into extinction by reason of obesity-induced immobility, infertility, sperm immotility and sterility or (b) epigenetically mutate – after reaching a tipping point of consciousness – into an enlightened, ungendered, asexual hermaphroditic species existing on a plane (and among a new biota on the planet) so spiritually elevated that the base instincts and appetites we are currently encumbered with will be sublimated into mystical states of bliss. In other words, Man will be either too fat to fuck or too blissed out to bother. Either way, Elijah is coming.

What evidence forms the basis of such theorising?

The consistent rise in childhood and adult obesity, diseases of the affluent and the growth in the fat industry – gastric reduction surgery, fat clinics, etc.; the preponderance of motorised buggies operated by gargantuan persons in supermarket aisles, airports and public spaces; the demand for oversized seats on passenger aeroplanes, the widening of aisles on said aeroplanes and the notable increase in width, girth and weight of flight attendants; the demand for the introduction of a sugar tax and other fat-reducing measures; the 50 per cent drop in human sperm count in the last forty years; the growth and widespread availability of online porn thus abrogating the need for sexual congress with another human being, thus-thus eliminating the possibility of reproduction; the growth and success rates of IVF and surrogacy; the no-longer-impossible-to-imagine scenario of *The Handmaid's Tale*; the evolutionary queering of humanity encompassing the rise in non-binary sexual orientation, the broadening of the sexual continuum, the shifting and fluid-ifying of gender reaching its possible culmination in a median gender akin to the hermaphrodite, where we will all be both male and female or neither, but very content; the human impulse for enlightenment, the human urge for the expansion of consciousness and/or altered states of consciousness; the contingent growth in consciousness programmes, self-awareness courses and the popularity of spirituality gurus and mentors. The proximity of Sisyphus's hour of descent as theorised by Albert Camus. The idea of the epiphany. The concept of the tipping point. The hypothetical phenom-enon of the hundredth monkey effect. Luke's own suscep-tibility to revelations.

Why does Luke not regard the idea of man's extinction as tragic?

Because it will mean the end of suffering. Because the natural order of every living thing is that it ends. Because it will be time for a new era and the turn of a new species to inhabit whatever survives of this planet. Because when the time comes, it will be the right thing to happen. Because man is not the centre of the universe. Because the universe has undergone previous cataclysmic changes and survived and there is no reason to suspect it will not continue to exist. Because man will return to the great consciousness of the universe and get a well-earned rest after all his travails.

* * *

The universe is conscious?

If we accept that the day is not far off when scientists will confirm that all sentient beings are conscious and indeed — and notwithstanding — that some degree of consciousness will be attributed to what we now regard as non-sentients (single-cell organisms, plants, organic matter), it is possible to imagine the universe as a great and continuous flow of consciousness, in the form of all matter, sentient and non-sentient, constantly in flux, moving and changing, forever dying and being reborn and transforming. In other words: the universe itself striving for greater consciousness. Luke is attracted to the ideas that philosopher David Chalmers postulates: first, that consciousness might be a fundamental feature or property of the universe, like space-time or energy or mass. And second, that consciousness might be universal: pan-psychism (pan meaning all and psyche meaning mind) — the idea that every system has some degree of consciousness. Not just humans and apes and dogs but also sea anemones and microbes and even sub-atomic particles. That microbes and photons might have some primitive element of subjective feeling, some precursor to consciousness, the first brief flickering of mind. And the further you advance along the continuum — from photon to sea-floor creature to mouse to man — the greater the consciousness. (And if we consider that 400 million years ago we swam in the same gene pool as creatures that later evolved into fish and birds (are not our hands converted fins?) then it's not such a stretch to imagine we might share consciousness with these and other distant kin.) So, all across the planet, trillions of minds are constantly generating vivid subjective experiences not unlike our own. Such ideas, while odd to the Western mind, are not inconsistent with Eastern philosophies where the human mind is seen as continuous with Nature.

How, now, is Luke alerted to his own altered state of consciousness?

When he stands, prompted by the need to relieve himself, the wall to his fore and the two walls to his sides tilt to the right and he tilts with them before dropping back down on the chair and reconsidering whether the walk to the bathroom is absolutely necessary. He stands again, touches the spot above his pubic bone, which, being sensitive, indicates a full bladder. Lily meows. He turns, walks, slips and falls.

In what posture does he find himself, after what period of time?

After undetermined hours and/or minutes, he finds himself prostrate not prone, semi-laterally inclined in a semi-foetal position, cold, stiff of neck, shoulder and back, with a pain in the thigh and the face. With a view of: the narrow leg of a chair, stout leg of the table. He chuckles. Stout. Mammy hated that. Used it on her enemies. That Bridget Kelly is getting very stout. Itchy face. Damp. Bloodied. Lily-clawed face.

* * *

What options of action or inaction present themselves to him?

To sleep or to wake, to rest or to rise.

Which does he choose?

Raising his upper body and placing his open right hand on the seat of a chair, he hoists himself upright, and stands still. Test of steadiness. The walls are tilting. Bursting to pee. Next stop, Kidney Junction. He puts one foot forward, then crosses the kitchen slowly to the sink. He pushes cups and cutlery aside. No harm, piss is sterile. He stands on his tippy toes and urinates. Such relief. The way ordinary things are undervalued. Why has he never read a good account of urination in a book?

How does he slake his thirst?

He takes a glass from the draining board, rinses it, fills it from the cold-water tap and drinks it in large glugs to the sound of the running water. Then he splashes water on his face.

As the water flows from the tap, of what is he reminded?

The reservoir at Roundwood. That he loves Leopold Bloom more than anyone else and he remembers well his first fall to the thrall.

Which was?

When Poldy fed the gulls. No, when Poldy said, 'Be kind to Athos.' No, that wasn't . . . When he saw Rudy's ghost

241

in an Eton suit and glass shoes and a little lambkin peeping out of his pocket.

How does Luke further slake his thirst?

With glass in hand, he crosses the kitchen, opens the lower-right press of the dresser and pours himself half a glass of Jameson whiskey. The first sip burns his tongue, his palate, then flows down his gullet. He emits a deep luxurious sigh. He steps towards the window, weaving a little. He rubs his chest. A touch of heartburn. The whiskey-blood swilling through his veins, rushing to the organs, the brain, the shrivelling corpuscles. Scorching the nerve endings. The cry of nerves, the worst cries in the world . . . Something to do with the Israelites, or Doomsday. He lifts his eyes to the clock: 1.25 . . . a.m. He drags a chair to the window, stands up on it and looks out at the full moon and the spilled down stars and experiences a moment of great clarity, expansion, increase. An inkling of revelation. On the cusp of something, maybe everything. He raises his face, opens his heart. He is high on the brow of the world now, in the universe's glow. On the moon's surface, his fellow-face. On the moon's surface, the marsh of dreams, the sea of rains, the gulf of dews, the river of fecundity.

What visible light attracts his vision, followed by what mental images?

The glancing light of the moon on the dark Sullane. Previous moons on previous water. The mind of the river winking into being. The first ever rain on Lougher, the soaking of ground, the splitting of earth at Meenganine, the spring-water rising, the pure, clean gathering stream; water trickling over stones, stream becoming river. The descent from Mullaghareirk; the dark of Duhallow; the silence of bogs; the changing of light; the rounding of bends, the turning of tides, the telluric vigour, the sublunary snow. Solitary wolves at Caoille tuned to the pitch of the earth; the caves at Duneevin; the artefacts at Lefanta; the first human settlements with men sheltering in trees; scavenging dogs and rats, harvesters with sickles and stones. St Carthage sailing upriver, his band of monks silenced by the vision of God's green beauty on the banks; plundering Vikings sailing upriver, silenced by the abundant possibilities. The monastic settlement, the Episcopal city, the glorious university when Oxford was still a cow-path. The massacre at Molana, the ruins at Rhincrew, the Templemichael Knights, the bloodbaths, the hooded hordes. The great houses on hills, the kitchen-hole drownings, the queuing of the scrofulous. The midstream islands, the mud-holes, the iron-ore mines, the weir at Rathmore. The boats and barges and schooners plying the waters with coal and corn, sand and gravel, salt and stone; the glint of salmon and lamprey and the heads of otters. The snow-white swans, the roosting birds. The river's longing, the *Illud Tempus.* The remembrance of water. The cosmological clock ticking time back to zero.

What thought now strikes him about the river?

Parataxis. All that is lost. All that is concealed. A sudden verticality in the horizontal. The primeval, medieval, coeval contents of the riverbed: drowned forests, ancient sap in the veins of ancient trees, eons of flora and fauna, incrustations of deep riches, of fossils and sand and silt, bipedal bones, teeth, fur and feathers. Calcious sediment of cold-blooded fish, warm-blooded mammals. Ancestral ooze: human, ovine, bovine, porcine, equine, lupine, corvine, canine, feline. The ancestral stock and sins of the multitudes. The soup of swamps and birdless forests before the age of man, before green-fringed banks and primitive ferns, before rocks and roots burst forth; before the river capture. The myriad of minute organisms below, above and beyond the perceptual register of man. The watery echoes of sonically different raindrops falling on multi-farious leaves. Wetlands, mudflats, flyways of migrating birds. The chorus of thrush and blackbird, the warblers high and hidden. The brown river, the bright air, the running sky, the hidden lairs, the habitat of millions. The otters, eels, minks and minnows looking back at wading, half-amphibian man.

Let him now elucidate the geological phenomenon that is the river capture.

When a river erodes the land and acquires the flow from another river or drainage system, usually below it, the first river is said to have captured the second in an act of piracy. The waters of the captured river are usurped by the captor and, at this point, the two become one. The causes: erosion, the superimposition of drainage, tectonic earth movements, landslides, the formation of natural dams, the movement of glaciers. The natural course of one river is altered, thwarted; the river departs its own grid of understanding, changes direction, flows on and enters the sea at an entirely different location. An eternal separation from the source ensues, a catastrophic event – the tail severed from the head, the worm cut in two. The bend in the river, the turn of the Sullane at the Inch, is the very point of capture, where, seventy million years ago, one river beheaded the other and the aggressor lost its way and cut down into the sandstone ridges and pirated the lower river and its route. A calamity for both rivers. But is not evolution punctuated by such calamities, such upheavals? Is not the sixth extinction near at hand?

What point of this explanation now confuses him?

Is it the low that takes the high or the high that takes the low? He is not sure. Who is the pirate, the aggressor – the lower or the upper river? His head starts to hurt. He had always thought the upper river – at a weakened, eroded point in its riverbed – had dropped down into the lower river or a lower, dry riverbed and, being the stronger one, had taken over the weaker lower flow. But the geological accounts, if he recalls them correctly, say the most common form of capture, called abstraction, occurs when the river that flows at a lower level cuts through the land dividing it from another river flowing *at a higher level*, causing that higher river to divert and rechannel itself. But how can river water cut through the land *above* it? He squints into the darkness outside . . . Once there were two. Now there is one. He holds his head in his hands . . . Poor river . . . A broken will, a spectral presence. A savage grace.

* * *

What epiphany does he now have concerning himself?

That the rug has been pulled. That his life has been thwarted. That his destiny has changed.

What epiphany does he have concerning water?

That it forbears, is ever patient, ever suffering, ever enduring. Long forgotten by the gods, ever in the service of man. Holy, seminal, giver and sustainer of life, sanitator, hydrator, germinator of life, quencher of thirsts and fires, cleanser of bodies and souls, gladdener of hearts, delighter of eyes. Docile accepter of Fate. Where once it carried memories from the realm of the dead to bubble up in poets, the pure hue of blue now carries human waste to the sewers and moderates nuclear reactors. That, since time immemorial, its collective experiences and memories in all its states (solid, liquid, gas and those derivative thereof), during all its cycles and circumambient journeys, in all causative occasions of joy, beauty, suffering (the glint of salmon in its rapids, the tranquil spring well, the swimmer's graceful stroke, the taking of life), and its presence at all natural, unnatural, scientific and unscientific actions, reactions and occurrences are all recorded and imprinted in its DNA. Bruised, battered, debased, diverted off course, forced through taps and pumps and pipes and turbines, catapulted through locks and dams and reservoirs and hydraulic colliders; endlessly recycled; swarmed with pathogens, sickened with leachate, bleachate, pesticides, insecticides, herbicides, with PCBs and TCEs; choked with micro-beads, fossil fuels, trash-entrapped gyres; subjected to sedimentation, acidification, chlorination, eutrophication, humiliation, anoxia, hypoxia, electrolysis; physically degraded, chemically altered, molecularly distorted, atomically perverted, metaphysically defiled. Used, abused, electrocuted ... poor exhausted water.

What compels him to leave the house?

The sudden conviction that he can perceive the mind of the river.

How does he go?

In the moonlight he runs. On the avenue he stumbles, falls, rises. On the road he walks towards the bridge of souls.

With what thought is he suddenly uplifted?

That he is walking along the riverbank into eternity.

How does he perceive the river?

As a seer, an augur of all that was and is to come.

How does he perceive the mind of the river?

Divided, exiled from itself, each half eternally mourning the loss of the other, looking south – nostalgic for the old route, for the whorls of old currents and stone pillows, the original neural way. Longing for reunion. Longing to be known. Longing to be understood.

*   *   *

Perched on the bridge, what does he see?

On the far bank, under a canopy of trees, two Charolais bulls hitched to a bronze plough. Above the trees, the church, the steeple. On the water, a trail of God's saliva, the glint of little fishes, the lustre of reeds and grasses. The tremolo of wind in the trees. The blood-wounds of the town and its hinterlands trickling into the river. People crowding to the water's edge. The river parting. The drenched world made visible: reeds and rushes, old boats and bicycles marinating in mud; bottles and cans and footballs and dolls and chicken bones and old mattresses and Madge Corcoran's yellow Escort and Milo Finnegan's VW Caddy. Madge and her baby, serene in the dark. Perished animals and the drownded dead, long accustomed to the depths now. All washed in the blood of the river. Tom Donoghue the county councillor in his suit and tie, Bina Rabbitte in her nurse's uniform; Conor Mahon with his 21st birthday badge still pinned to his shirt; Jimbo McInerney still weeping for his horse, and Paudge Fleming and Bridget Flynn and Paddy Boyle and Ulick Veale and Ulick Vesey among the swarming souls. And on the surface, oblivious to it all, anglers angling and families boating and jet-skiers skiing and skinny-legged herons at the Inch and tractors barrelling over the bridge into town and trucks nosing up Main Street and Dilly Madden on the footpath cursing them all and Bun Heapy in from Botany for a barrel of gas and Paddy the Vet above with Paddy the Gas O'Donnell pulling a calf as their sons walk hand in hand into the river at Drumona and Paddy the Gas asking Paddy the Vet, Is it the Euphrates, Paddy, that's the fourth river of Paradise?

What spectacle, in need of his *contemplatio, consideratio* and *designatio*, appears in the sky above the Inch?

A polygonal shape, a celestial templum, a sacred imago hovering above the water. Attended by a flight of birds, a trail of clouds, an eagle with the liver of a sacrificed goat in its beak. At the exact point of the river capture the heavenly templum aligns its axes with the river's stars, lowers itself over the water, fixes itself to the river mundus, and is inaugurated. *Ego te inauguro.*

In this full and absolute moment what is revealed to him?

His life was justified.

As he enters the river, what does he foresee?

His soul in repose in an aqueous kingdom. The river in repose. Man and nature in perfect harmony. Time and space in perfect symmetry. The world a work of art.

YESTERDAY I SAW Andy Mullins coming out of the post office after collecting his dole, then hurrying along Main Street to the Tavern Bar. As he passed SuperValu the glass doors slid open. I wanted to burst out laughing. What if mankind has been on the wrong track for thousands of years? What if Aristotle and Plato took a wrong turn in assuming that everything that happens has a purpose, instead of accepting the free movement of atoms in space? What if the theosophists were right and the purpose of reincarnation is to test and refine the soul until it emerges as pure spirit?

Last week I took Lily to the vet to be spayed. She had never been in a pet carrier, so I covered it with a blanket to keep her calm. That's how they brought the Duke's horses out of the fire years ago. If they can't see, they won't panic. Rachel, the vet, is a chirpy woman of about forty. She was wearing a blood-stained white coat, tight across her middle. Later that afternoon, she phoned to tell me that when she opened the carrier Lily leapt past her and bolted out the back door. She's probably nearby, she said. If you come before five, there's a good chance she'll come out of hiding.

We now know that the structural memory of water persists on a picosecond timescale. Is it not possible that the human measurement of time and the human experience of the time-space continuum differs from water's measurement of time and water's experience of the time-space continuum, and that a picosecond in human time equates to a greater measure in water time? Or that water time advances not just in a forward-future motion but backwards and outwards, too, in a radiating nexus of pan-aqueous interactions and ripples that follow their own bliss? Is it not possible that we are wildly underestimating the ways in which water experiences its life?

Some mornings when I'm getting dressed or when I turn my head suddenly towards the window, I get a whiff of the river off myself. It is a woody, mushroomy smell that I can almost taste and I bury my nose in my upper arm or in the angle of my elbow and sniff myself.

I was euphoric that night, as if the thing I had always been waiting for had finally arrived, as if I was about to be married. The moon's glow was on everything. I pushed off and dropped vertically into the water. In that moment I could see myself gliding gracefully to the bottom, as if I was looking down from above. I foresaw it all: a beautiful descent, eyes slowly opening and closing, arms raised and hands joined as if in prayer, the muted sounds and slow-motion swoon of an underwater dream. Then, my serene repose in a hole in the riverbed.

But that is not what happened. As soon as I broke the skin of the river, a vicious wave pummelled me with fragments of foam and debris. I lurched and banked and from my brain and then my stomach came the irresistible urge for violence. I banked again and turned and thrashed the foaming waves and dived under into a strange, viscous world lit up by a green watery light. I could feel vague presences and a low humming vibration, as if music was reaching me from a different sphere.

And then came a moment of sublime clarity. Lured by the light and the quivering frequency of the water I felt my soul approaching the soul of the river, entering synchrony with the tremulous water, and, lucid, tranquil and in thrall to the mysterious conjunction and the radiance of water, I let my soul commingle and become the river's dream.

What I remember next was the sound of water lapping and faint cries echoing through it. I was stretched out on the riverbank, my face on wet reeds, my pulse beating in my ears. I raised my head and, with half-open eyes, I saw the dawn. In the distance I heard Lily crying. I lifted my gaze to the green wet world of the Inch, with the river running and willows dipping and the earth's breath around me. My head fell again and my eyes closed. Again Lily's cries broke through, insistent. I hauled myself to my knees, crawled over soft mounds of moss. Dazed, damp, shivering, I stood on the riverbank and opened my mouth and inhaled the cold air of the atmosphere. I could no longer doubt I was alive. I stumbled onto the road and walked towards Lily's cries. At the bottom of the avenue she came bounding towards me and leapt into my arms.

I walked on. The sun was rising in the east. I could feel Lily's heartbeat, very close to the surface. I stopped in the middle of the road and looked up at Ellen's house on the hill. I waited for ten or twenty – or maybe more – seconds. Then she appeared at the window and raised her hand and waved. I waved back and something passed between us. I walked back the way I had come and when I turned in the avenue a small cloud of vapour appeared before me and with it came the thought that the signature of all things is inscribed in water.

I sat in the vet's back yard that night Lily went missing. In the darkness the bushes and trees took on ominous shapes. I could sense Lily's presence. I was barely breathing, alert to every sound, willing her back. I thought I saw her on the wall a few times, her silhouette. A rustle in the bushes then and a flock of crows rose out of the trees. I thought of Ezra Pound imprisoned in his wire cage near Pisa, counting birds on distant wires to stay sane. I thought of the experiment on swallows to determine the energy costs of birds' flight and how, before releasing the birds seventy kilometres from home, the scientists passed a thread through their nostrils and tied their beaks shut.

By midnight I could feel Lily's presence waning. I could feel myself moving towards a more impersonal, non-physical view of the world. I could sense the universe itself becoming conscious.

Last night I dreamt I was walking along a Paris street with Joyce. He was animated in his talk, spritely in his walk. You are my metaphysical magnet, he said. Then he explained his books to me. *Ulysses* is Hell, he said, Hell being the state of the soul fixated upon earthly experiences. *Finnegans Wake* is Purgatory – a halfway house before people became attached to themselves. And my next book, he said, will be Paradise – a pure, simple heaven, my final achievement.

Today I made a mental list of the invisible yet enduring rivers of the underworld. I thought of my own riparian existence. I thought: this is my only available body. I thought of the birds in flight with their beaks tied, and the little bull calves in New Zealand, and Lily, alone out there some-where. I feel such liquid love in my arms for her now. I feel such pity for water now. I'd like to talk to Poldy now.

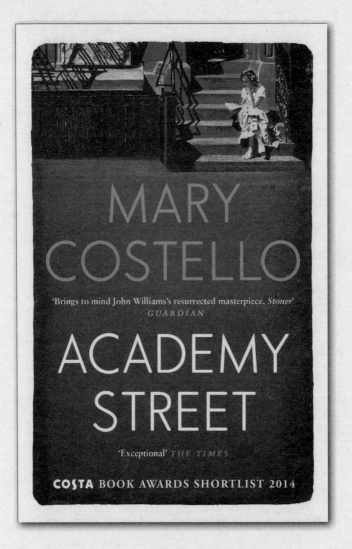

'Packed with emotional intensity'
Guardian

CANON█GATE

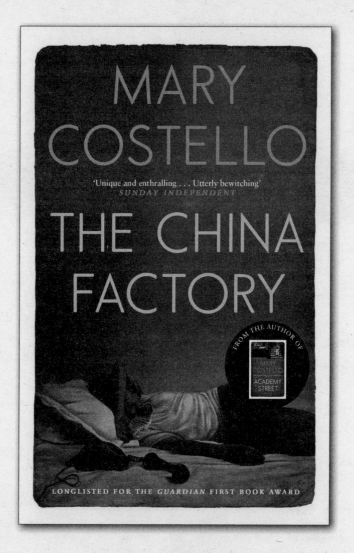

MARY
COSTELLO

'Unique and enthralling . . . Utterly bewitching'
SUNDAY INDEPENDENT

THE CHINA
FACTORY

FROM THE AUTHOR OF

MARY
COSTELLO
ACADEMY
STREET

LONGLISTED FOR THE *GUARDIAN* FIRST BOOK AWARD

'Simply a masterpiece'
Irish Independent

CANON▌GATE